THE LION
Storyteller
AWESOME
BOOK OF STORIES

Text copyright © 1998, 2002, 2009, 2011, 2016 Bob Hartman
Illustrations copyright © 2009, 2011 Krisztina Kállai Nagy
This edition copyright © 2016 Lion Hudson

The right of Bob Hartman to be identified as the author and of Krisztina Kállai Nagy to be identified as the illustrator of this work has been asserted by them in accordance with the Copyright, Designs and Patents Act 1988.

Published by Lion Children's Books
an imprint of
Lion Hudson plc
Wilkinson House,
Jordan Hill Road,
Oxford OX2 8DR, England
www.lionhudson.com/lionchildrens

ISBN 978 0 7459 7636 5
e-ISBN 978 0 7459 6799 8 (*Bedtime Book*; text-only)
e-ISBN 978 0 7459 6798 1 (*Animal Tales*; text-only)

First edition 2016

The stories in this book were first published in *The Lion Storyteller Bedtime Book* and *The Lion Storyteller Book of Animal Tales*.

Acknowledgments
Cover image: © angel_1978/iStock

A catalogue record for this book is available from the British Library

Printed and bound in China, April 2016, LH06

THE LION Storyteller AWESOME BOOK OF STORIES

Retold by Bob Hartman
Illustrations by Krisztina Kállai Nagy

LION
CHILDREN'S

Contents

Introduction

It's hard to tell a story you don't love.

That's my experience, anyway. Some stories grab hold of you by the collar and shout, "Tell me! Tell me, please."

And others are just, "Meh, if you have to tell me, fair enough. But I don't really see us in a long-term relationship, here."

When I wrote the two books that are bundled together in this collection, I spent hours in the bowels of the Pittsburgh Public Libraries, gathering up collections of stories from around the world. Then I spent hours more, in my study, reading what I'd gathered and letting the stories speak.

Some tales, like "The Mouse and the Lion", leaped and roared at me. Others, like "Tortoise Brings Food", crept up on me (slowly and carefully – when you read it, you'll see). And Danny and Granny and "The Big, Soft, Fluffy Bed" jumped up and down and made all kinds of noises until I paid attention. They have all become lifelong friends.

I have gathered the stories in this collection from every part of the globe. Some of them may be familiar to you. But I hope that many more will be new – that you will share my delight in discovering them for the first time and also come to appreciate, as I did, how similar our dreams and values are, regardless of culture, nature or race.

I have also consciously chosen stories that I believe encourage the very best human traits. I really think that stories can encourage children to be more kind or gentle or compassionate – that's another of my hopes for this book.

I also hope that, as you read these stories yourself, or read them to the children in your life, they will become your friends as well as mine. I can't guarantee it, of course. Stories don't work like that. But I'm happy to have the chance to introduce them to you – the stories in this collection – and see what happens.

Perhaps you will make a few friends as well.

Bob Hartman

The Mouse and the Lion

The mouse skittered left.

The mouse skittered right.

The mouse skittered round a rock and under a leaf and past the dark, wide mouth of a cave.

And then the little mouse stopped.

Something had grabbed his tail.

The mouse wrinkled his nose and twitched his whiskers and turned around. The something was a lion!

"You're not even a snack," the lion yawned, as he picked up the mouse and dangled him over his mouth. "But you'll be tasty, nonetheless."

"I'm much more than a snack!" the little mouse squeaked. "I'm brave and I'm clever and I'm stronger than you think. And I'm sure that if you let me go I will be useful to you one day. Much more useful than a bit of bone and fur that you will gobble up and then forget."

The lion roared with laughter, and the little mouse was blown about by his hot breath.

"Useful? To me?" the lion chuckled. "I doubt it. But you are brave, I'll give you that. And cheeky, to boot. So I'll let you go. But watch your tail. I may not be so generous again."

The mouse skittered left.

The mouse skittered right.

The mouse skittered away as quickly as he could, and disappeared into the woods.

Hardly a week had passed when the lion wandered out of his cave in search of food.

The lion looked left.

The lion looked right.

But when the lion leaped forwards, he fell into a hunter's snare!

The ropes wrapped themselves around him. He was trapped.

Just then the little mouse came by.

"I told you I could be useful," the little mouse squeaked. "Now I shall prove it to you."

The lion was in no mood for jokes. He could hear the hunter's footsteps. "How?" he whispered. "How can you help me, now?"

"Be still," said the mouse. "And let me do my work."

The mouse began to gnaw. And to nibble. And to chew. And soon the ropes were weak enough for the lion to snap them with a shrug of his powerful shoulders.

So, just as the hunter appeared in the clearing, the lion leaped away into the forest, with his new friend clinging to his curly mane.

They returned to the cave as the sun fell behind the hills.

"Thank you, my friend," said the lion to the mouse. "You are indeed clever and brave, and you have been more useful than I could ever have imagined. From now on, you have nothing to fear from me."

The little mouse smiled.

Then he skittered left.

And he skittered right.

And he skittered off into the night.

11

Silly Jack

On Monday morning, Jack's mother sent him off to work for the carpenter. Jack worked hard, and at the end of the day the carpenter gave him a shiny new penny.

Jack carried the penny home, tossing it in the air as he went. But as he crossed the little bridge over the narrow brook, he dropped the penny and lost it in the water below.

When he told her, Jack's mother shook her head. "You silly boy," she sighed, "you should have put the penny in your pocket. You must remember that tomorrow."

On Tuesday morning, Jack's mother sent him off to work for the farmer. Jack worked very hard, and at the end of the day the farmer gave him a jug of milk.

Jack remembered his mother's words, and carefully slipped the jug of milk into his big coat pocket. But as he walked home, the milk splashed and splooshed and spilled out of the jug and all over Jack's fine coat.

When he told her, Jack's mother shook her head. "You silly boy," she sighed, "you should have carried the jug on your head. You must remember that tomorrow."

On Wednesday morning, Jack's mother sent him off to work for the baker. Jack worked very hard, and at the end of the day, the baker gave him a beautiful black cat.

Jack remembered his mother's words, and carefully sat the cat on his head. But on the way home, the cat was frightened, leaped from Jack's head into a nearby tree, and refused to come down.

When he told her, Jack's mother shook her head. "You silly boy," she sighed, "you should have tied a string around the cat's collar and pulled it home behind you. You must remember that tomorrow."

On Thursday morning, Jack's mother sent him off to work for the butcher. Jack worked very hard, and at the end of the day, the butcher gave him a huge leg of lamb.

Jack remembered his mother's words, tied a string around the meat, and pulled it home behind him. But by the time he got home, the meat was covered with dirt, and good for nothing but to be thrown away.

When he told her, Jack's mother shook her head. "You silly, silly boy," she sighed. "Don't you know you should have carried it home on your shoulder? Promise me you will remember that tomorrow."

Jack promised, and on Friday morning, his mother sent him off to work for the man who ran the stables. Jack worked very hard, and at the end of the day, the man gave him a donkey!

Jack looked at the donkey. Jack remembered his promise. Then he swallowed hard, picked that donkey up, and hoisted it onto his shoulders!

On the way home, Jack passed by the house of a rich man – a rich man whose beautiful daughter had never laughed in all her life.

But when she saw poor, silly Jack giving that donkey a ride, she giggled, she chuckled, then she burst out laughing, right there and then.

The rich man was delighted, and gave Jack his daughter's hand in marriage, and a huge fortune besides.

When he told her, Jack's mother didn't shake her head. No, she hugged him and she kissed him and she shouted, "Hooray!" and she never ever called him "silly" again.

The Girl Who Played With the Stars

Once upon a time, there lived
a little girl who wanted one thing
and one thing only – to play with
the stars in the sky!

Every night, before she fell asleep,
she would stare out of her bedroom window at the stars dancing above her,
and wish that someday she might dance with them.

One night, she decided to make her wish come true. So she crept from her
bedroom, down the stairs, and out of the front door. And she set off to find
her way to the stars.

The moon was full. The night was warm and bright. And it wasn't long
before she spotted the stars – reflected in the water of a little pond.

"Excuse me," she whispered to the pond, "can you tell me how to get
to the stars?"

"That's easy," the pond rippled and shook, "the stars come and shine
in my eyes on most nights, so brightly in fact that I have trouble sleeping.
If you want to find them, you're welcome to jump in."

And so the little girl did. She swam and swam around that little pond,
but she could not find a single star. So she climbed sadly out again, said
goodbye to the pond, and set off, dripping, down the path.

Before long, she came to a little field. And there were the stars, dancing
like tiny lights in the dewy grass. And dancing with them were the fairies –
clapping their hands and beating their wings to the sound of harp and pipe
and drum.

"Excuse me," she called to the little people, "I want more than anything to play with the stars. Do you mind if I join you?"

"Of course not," the fairies called back. "Come and dance with us as long as you like."

And so the little girl danced. She danced round and round till she could hardly stand. But she never danced with any stars, no, not one. For the stars were not there at all. They were nothing more than reflections in the wet grass.

When the little girl realized this, she fell to the ground sobbing. And the fairies stopped their dancing and hovered round her.

"I've swum and I've swum," she sobbed. "I've danced and I've danced. And still I have not found the stars."

The fairies felt sorry for the little girl, so they did what they could. They gave her a little riddle.

"Ask Four Feet to carry you to No Feet At All," they told her. "Then ask No Feet At All to carry you to the Stairs Without Steps. And there you will find the stars."

The fairies went back to their dancing, and the little girl went on her way. Soon she met a horse.

"Excuse me," she asked, as politely as she could, "I'm on my way to the stars. Could you give me a ride?"

The horse neighed and shook his shaggy head. "I cannot help you," he explained. "For I am here to help the fairies and the fairies only."

"Ah," the little girl smiled, "then you must be Four Feet. The fairies told me about you. They said that I must ask you to take me to No Feet At All."

"Well, that's different!" the horse snorted. "Climb aboard, and we shall be there in no time." And off they went, through the forests and over the fields – hooves hammering and hair blowing, west and west and west, until they reached the sea.

"I can carry you no further," the horse explained. "You must wait here on the beach for No Feet At All."

15

The little girl had so many questions. Who was No Feet At All? What did he look like? How would she find him? But before she could ask a single question, the horse turned and galloped away. The little girl looked up into the sky. The stars were as far away as ever. And she was lost and all alone.

Suddenly, however, something went splash. Then splish-splash. Then splish-splash-splish. The girl looked into the sea, and there was a fish – a huge fish, a massive fish, a great giant of a fish.

"Could it be?" she wondered. And so she called, "No Feet At All? Is that you, No Feet At All?" And the great fish leaped out of the water and landed near the edge of the beach.

"Where shall I carry you, my dear?" asked the fish.

"To the Stairs Without Steps," said the little girl. And off they went, fins flapping, night-dress dripping, slicing through the salty waves, west and west and west. And then the fish just stopped.

"We're here," he gurgled, "at the Stairs Without Steps."

But the little girl could see nothing at all.

"Step off my back," the fish insisted. "It will be all right."

So the little girl stepped – stepped off the fish's back and into what looked for all the world like a vast and endless sea. But before her foot could touch

the water, a pure white gull flew under it. She stepped higher, and there was another gull, and so she stepped higher still. And with every step, a gull was there to hold her. When she had climbed too high for the gulls to fly, the clouds took over, and step by cloudy step they carried her at last to the land of the stars!

The stars reached out their warm and shiny arms to welcome her, and she spent the rest of that night dancing their sparkling dances and playing their golden games. When the little girl finally grew tired, they wrapped her up in a cloud and sent her off to sleep.

"Come again any time!" the stars said, their eyes twinkling, their faces shining.

The girl dreamed of fairies and night wind and stars. But when she awoke, she was back in her room and the cloud beneath her head was nothing more than her own soft pillow. Had it all been a dream, nothing more than a dream? Then why was the hem of her night-dress damp? And why did her hair smell of cold, salty air? And where had the horsehair come from, which she clutched in her little hand?

The little girl smiled, and pulled the blankets tight up to her chin. Then she made another wish, and shut her eyes, and set off to dream.

Three Months' Night

The pine trees stood tall. The mountains behind them stood taller still. And, in a clearing in the midst of the trees, the animals gathered together.

Their leader, the coyote, perched on a wide flat rock and howled, "A-Woo," so everyone could hear.

"My friends," he called, "we have a decision to make. Think hard. Take your time. And then tell me. How long should each day be?"

The animals looked at one another. They grunted and squealed and roared. Such a hard decision! Then they became quiet, and set to thinking.

After a long while, the grizzly bear raised one fat, furry paw and slowly wiggled his four sharp claws.

"I think…" he yawned. "I think that each day should be three months long. And the same with each night. That way…" he yawned again, "we could get all the sleep we need."

The animals were shocked by the bear's answer, and the grunting and squealing and roaring started all over again. But it was the chipmunk who spoke up most loudly.

"Don't be ridiculous!" he chattered. "If I slept for three months, I would starve to death! I say we keep things just as they are – with one day followed by one night."

The owl and the weasel and many of the other animals agreed. But the grizzly stood his ground, and soon the woods were filled with the noise of the animals' argument.

"Enough. A-Woo. Enough!" the coyote howled. "We will settle this matter with a contest. Chipmunk, you must repeat, over and over again, the words, 'One day, one night', for that is what you want.

"As for you, Grizzly Bear, you must say,

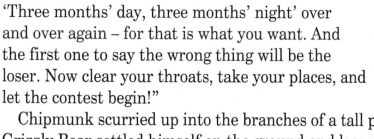

'Three months' day, three months' night' over and over again – for that is what you want. And the first one to say the wrong thing will be the loser. Now clear your throats, take your places, and let the contest begin!"

Chipmunk scurried up into the branches of a tall pine tree. Grizzly Bear settled himself on the ground and leaned against the trunk. And then they started.

"One day, one night, one day, one night," the chipmunk chattered, faster and faster in his squeaky little voice.

"Three months' day, three months' night," the bear repeated slowly, but he was sleepy and tired and found it hard to concentrate.

"One day, one night, one day, one night, one day, one night," the chipmunk chattered faster than ever, and it was all the bear could do to hear his own grizzly voice. And that's when it happened. Instead of saying, "Three months' day, three months' night," the poor bear mumbled, "One day, one night." And the contest was over!

"Chipmunk has won. A-Woo!" the coyote howled. "And so it shall be one day and one night forevermore."

But the grizzly bear refused to give in. "I need three months' sleep," he growled, "and I intend to get it!"

He stood up and swung an angry paw at Chipmunk. But Chipmunk darted away, so that the bear's claws left nothing but four long scratches down his back. Then the bear sulked away, hid himself in a cave, and settled down for a long winter's sleep.

And, to this day, every chipmunk bears the marks of Grizzly's claws on his back. And each winter every grizzly goes to sleep for a three months' night.

Arion and the Dolphin

When Arion played his harp, everybody listened.

The Greek men put down their tools. The Greek women put down their pots. The Greek children put down their toys. And even the birds in the air, the animals in the field, and the fish in the sea stopped their screeching and scratching and splashing to listen to his beautiful songs.

Arion was hardly more than a boy, but no one played the harp more skilfully or sang so sweetly. The king himself had said so! And so it came as no surprise when Arion decided to leave his homeland and sail for the island of Sicily, hoping to find fame and fortune there as well.

It happened, of course.

When Arion played, everybody listened.

The Sicilian men put down their tools. The Sicilian women put down their pots. The Sicilian children put down their toys. And, along with the birds and the fish and the animals, they marvelled at the Greek lad's lovely songs.

The people of Sicily showered Arion with silver and gold and jewels. So it was as a rich young man that he boarded a Greek ship and set sail for home.

The captain of the ship knew all about Arion, but he cared little for music and a great deal for gold. So, when they had sailed far from shore, he made his sailors grab hold of Arion and drag him to the side of the ship.

"You are a rich young man, Arion," the captain laughed, "but not for long. My men are going to kill you and throw your body overboard, and we shall have your treasure!"

"Dear captain," Arion sighed, "if your heart is set on ending my life and stealing my fortune, there is nothing I can do to stop you. But at least grant me one wish before I die. Let me play my harp one last time."

The captain shrugged. "What harm can it do?" And he tossed the musician his harp.

Arion began to play. Arion began to sing. And, just as he expected, everybody listened.

The sailors put down their ropes. The captain put down his sword. Even the gulls above and the fish below stopped their swooping and swimming to listen to the lad's last beautiful song.

But, just as the song was about to finish, Arion grabbed his harp tightly and flung himself from the boat and into the bright blue sea.

"Don't worry about him, lads," the captain called. "No one could swim to shore from here. The sharks will see to that. Now, let's have a look at his treasure!"

Arion, meanwhile, began to sink, for he could not hold on to his harp and swim. Down and down, deeper and deeper, sank the poor singer.

And then, suddenly, he stopped! And instead of sinking further, he began to rise, up and up, higher and higher, until his head popped out of the waves and he could breathe again!

Arion looked down and was surprised to find himself sitting on the back of a dolphin – a dolphin who had heard Arion's beautiful song and was determined that such a singer should not drown.

Arion wrapped his legs round the dolphin's sides. He wrapped one arm round its neck. And the dolphin carried Arion through the waves, all the way back to Greece.

Arion thanked his new friend and waved goodbye. And the dolphin leaped up out of the sea, clapping and clacking his farewell. Then Arion tucked his harp under his arm and set off to see the king.

When he arrived at the palace, the king was busy – in fact, he was talking with the very sailors who had stolen Arion's treasure. So Arion asked the guard to keep silent, while he slipped quietly behind a stone pillar to listen.

"It was a sorry thing, Your Majesty," the captain explained. "The storm came upon us like a fierce beast and, before we could do a thing, poor Arion and his treasure were swept overboard."

The king sadly shook his head. "I can't believe it," he sighed. "I shall never hear that beautiful voice and harp again."

But just as the king finished, the sound of a harp came floating out from the back of the hall. And it was followed by Arion's beautiful voice.

The guards put down their spears. The king put down his royal staff. And the sailors fell trembling to their knees.

Arion slipped out from behind the pillar and walked slowly towards the throne. The king clapped his hands for joy.

"You're alive!" he shouted. "You did not drown! What power saved you from the terrible storm?"

"There was no storm, Your Majesty." Arion explained. And then he told the king all about the captain's wicked plan.

Soldiers were sent to the ship and, sure enough, they found Arion's treasure. So the captain and his crew were packed off to prison. Arion's treasure was returned to him. And the king ordered his sculptors to make a statue of a boy on the back of a dolphin – in memory of Arion and his amazing rescue.

Rabbit and Tiger Save the World

Tiger was huge! Tiger was fierce! Tiger had sharp claws, even sharper teeth, and beautiful orange-and-black striped skin. But, for all his good looks, Tiger was not very clever.

Rabbit, on the other hand, was small. And not very scary at all. Rabbit had long ears, a powder-puff tail and a brain that was every bit as quick as his long, strong legs.

Tiger wanted to eat Rabbit, more than anything else in the world!

And, more than anything else in the world, Rabbit did not want to be eaten!

One day, as Rabbit was out nibbling daisies for his dinner, Tiger surprised him. Tiger chased Rabbit through the jungle and across the fields and into a deep, rocky ravine.

There was no way out. Rabbit was trapped! So he stopped using his quick legs and used his quick brain instead. He threw himself, arms outstretched, against a huge boulder at the end of the ravine, and waited for Tiger to catch up.

"Now I've got you!" Tiger roared. "And I can almost taste the rabbit stew."

"You may eat me if you like," said Rabbit, slowly, "but first you will have to tear me away from this boulder I am holding up."

"And what would be wrong with that?" asked the puzzled Tiger.

"Well, this boulder holds up the whole world," answered Rabbit. "I saw it start to roll away, and fortunately I was here to stop it. But if I move away from here, it will start rolling again – and take the whole world with it!"

"Oh dear!" said Tiger, "I had no idea."

"I'll tell you what," grinned Rabbit. "Why don't you hold it up for me and let me run and get some help."

"Certainly," said the worried Tiger. "We don't want the world to roll away!"

So Rabbit ran. But he didn't run for help. He ran straight to his rabbit hidey-hole, laughing all the way – and safe at last.

The Shepherd and the Clever Princess

Princess Vendla could speak any language. Any language in the world!

German, French.

Italian, Polish.

Chinese, Zulu, English.

She could understand them all.

Her father, the king, was proud of her. So proud, in fact, that he set a challenge for all the young men in his kingdom.

"If you want to marry my daughter," he announced, "you must first speak to her in a language she does not understand. Succeed, and she shall be your bride. Fail, and you shall be thrown into the sea!"

Many men tried. Wise men. Rich men. Handsome men. But, sadly, each and every one of them ended up in the sea.

And then, one day, Timo the shepherd boy decided that it was time to find a wife.

"They say the princess is quite pretty," he thought. "So I shall take up the king's challenge and make her my bride."

Now Timo was neither wise, nor rich, nor handsome. In fact, he was a dreamer, who wandered through the forests and across the fields chatting with the birds and whispering to the animals.

Timo set off for the king's palace. He hadn't gone far when he heard a noise – a chippery, chirping noise – the cry of a little bird. But the noise wasn't falling down from somewhere high in the trees. No, it was leaping up from somewhere on the ground.

Timo followed the noise. He brushed away branches and old, dead leaves. And soon he found it – a sad young sparrow with a badly broken wing.

"Poor little fellow," Timo said. "You're lucky you haven't been gobbled up by a fox or a cat. Why don't you ride with me for a while?"

And Timo picked up the little sparrow and set him gently in his big leather pouch.

Timo walked a little further and soon he heard another noise – a scritchity, scratching noise that could come only from a squirrel.

"I'm caught. I'm caught in a trap!" the little squirrel chattered. "Won't somebody please help me?"

Timo was there in a minute. He loosened the sharp wire from around the squirrel's leg. Then he picked him up and put him in his pouch next to the sparrow.

"You can rest there," he whispered to the squirrel, "until your leg is better."

Timo started off for the king's palace, once again, but it wasn't long before he heard yet another noise – a crawing, caw-cawing noise, high above his head.

"What's the matter, Mr Crow?" Timo called.

"I have lost my wife!" cawed the crow. "The king's hunters were out in the woods, and I fear they have taken her. I have been flying in circles for hours and I cannot find her."

"Why not come with me?" said Timo. "I am going to the king's palace this very day. You can hop into my pouch and ride along."

The tired crow gladly accepted Timo's offer, and before long, the shepherd boy and his secret companions were at the palace gates.

"Who goes there?" shouted the watchman.

"It's Timo, the shepherd boy. I have come to marry the princess."

"You mean you've come to be tossed into the sea!" the watchman laughed. "Men wiser and richer than yourself have found their way there already."

"Perhaps," Timo nodded. "But they did not know what I know – a language that Princess Vendla will not understand."

The watchman let Timo into the palace, and then led him to the king.

"Your Majesty," Timo bowed, "I have come to take up your challenge. I believe I know a language that your daughter will not understand."

The king could not keep himself from laughing.

"But you are just a poor shepherd boy," he chuckled. "And my daughter has studied every language in the world! The sea is very cold at this time of year. Are you sure you want to accept my challenge?"

"I do," Timo nodded. "I want to see the princess."

The king called for his daughter, and she was the most beautiful girl young Timo had ever seen. He bowed to the princess, then he reached his hand into his leather pouch and gently scratched the little sparrow's head.

"Chip-chirp-chippery-chirp," said the sparrow.

Timo looked at Princess Vendla. "Can you tell me what that means?" he asked.

Princess Vendla looked very worried. "Why, no," she said slowly, "I can't."

"It means: 'Thank you for rescuing me, Timo. My wing is much better now.'"

Timo reached his hand into his pouch again, and this time he tickled the squirrel under his furry chin.

"Scrick-scrack-scrickity-scrack," said the squirrel. And again the princess could only shake her head.

"This is an easy one," said Timo. "It means: 'Thank you for the ride and for saving me from the hunter's trap.'"

Timo reached his hand once more into his pouch, but before he could nudge the crow, the king stood up and shouted, "Enough! I am ashamed of you, daughter. I gave you the finest teachers in the world and yet this ignorant shepherd boy knows more than you!"

"I'm sorry, Father," the princess sobbed, "perhaps I am not so clever as you thought."

"Oh no, princess," said Timo. "You are very clever indeed. Clever enough to admit that there are things you still must learn. That is the beginning of real wisdom, and I admire you all the more for it."

The king smiled when he heard these words. He announced that Timo and Vendla should be married that very day, and everyone in the palace cheered.

So it was that Timo came to live at the palace. And, with the help of the sparrow, the squirrel, the crows, and all his other woodland friends, he taught Princess Vendla the language of the animals.

And they all lived happily ever after.

27

Tortoise Brings Food

The sun was hot. The earth was dry. There had been no rain for many months. And now there was no food. The animals were very hungry.

Lion, king of all the beasts, called his thin and tired friends together under the shade of a tall, gnarled tree.

"The legends say this is a magic tree," he roared, "which will give us all the food we need – if only we can say its secret name. But there is only one person who knows that name – the old man who lives at the top of the mountain."

"Then we must go to him," trumpeted Elephant, "as quickly as we can! Before we all starve to death."

"I'll go," said Tortoise, slowly. And everyone just stopped and stared.

"Don't be silly," roared Lion. "It would take you for ever! No, we shall send Hare to find the name of the tree. He will be back in no time."

Hare hurried up the side of the mountain, his long ears blown back against the side of his head. He leaped. He scampered. He raced. And soon he was face to face with the old man.

"Please tell me the name of the magic tree," he begged. "The animals are very hungry."

The old man looked. The old man listened. And then the old man said one word and one word only: "Uwungelema."

"Thank you," panted Hare. And then he hurried back down the mountainside.

He leaped. He scampered. He raced. All the while repeating to himself the name of the magic tree: "Uwungelema, Uwungelema, Uwungelema."

But, just as he reached the bottom of the mountain, Hare hurried –

28

CRASH! – right into the
side of a huge anthill, and
knocked himself silly.

So silly, in fact, that by the time he
had staggered back to all the other animals,
he had completely forgotten the name of the
magic tree!

"We must send someone else," roared Lion. "Someone
who will not forget."

"I'll go," said Tortoise, again.

And this time, the other animals laughed.

"We'll have starved to death by the time you get back," chuckled
Lion. "No, we shall send Elephant."

Elephant hurried up the side of the mountain, his long trunk
swaying back and forth. He tramped. He trundled. He tromped.
And soon he was face to face with the old man.

"Please tell me the name of the magic tree," he begged. "The animals
are very hungry."

The old man looked puzzled. "I have already told Hare," he said. "But
I suppose I can tell you, too." And then he said that word: "Uwungelema."

"Thank you," panted Elephant. And then he hurried back down the
mountainside.

He tramped. He trundled. He tromped. All the while repeating to himself
that secret name: "Uwungelema, Uwungelema, Uwungelema." But, just
like Hare, he was in such a hurry that he failed to notice the anthill. And he
too stumbled – CRASH! – right into its side, knocking himself so silly that
he, too, forgot the secret name.

"This is ridiculous!" roared Lion. "Is there no one who can remember
a simple name?"

"I can," said Tortoise quietly.

And the other animals just shook their heads.

"Enough!" roared Lion. "It looks as if I shall have to do it myself."

So Lion hurried up the hill and talked to the old man. But on the
way back he, too, stumbled into the anthill and staggered back
to the others, having forgotten the name completely.

"What shall we do now?" moaned Giraffe.

"It's not impossible at all!" the frog bar-durped. "I'll tell you how to do it, if you'll promise me one thing."

"Anything!" Polly sobbed.

"You must do everything I ask of you for one whole night! Bar-durp."

Well, it seemed a strange thing to ask, but Polly was desperate. And besides, this frog didn't even know where she lived.

"All right," Polly agreed. "Now tell me, please."

"Bar-durp. Take some moss and some old leaves and jam them into the holes. Then the water won't leak out."

Polly did what the frog suggested and, sure enough, it worked!

"Thank you!" she smiled. "You've saved my life!"

"Bar-durp," the frog smiled back. "Just remember your promise." And he did a fat bellyflop back into the water.

Polly hurried home, and her stepmother was so amazed that, for once, she didn't even try to find something wrong with Polly's work. But, later that night, as Polly was finishing her dinner, there was a knock at the door.

"Polly," her father called. "There's a frog here to see you."

Polly swallowed the mouthful of food she was chewing, then rose slowly and walked to the front door. The fat, friendly frog was dripping all over the front mat.

"So it's Polly, is it?" croaked the frog. "Nice name. Do you mind if I – bar-durp – come in?"

Polly minded very much. But she also remembered her promise. So she invited him in, and then added, very quickly, "But we're in the middle of dinner."

"Oh that's all right," the frog said, flicking out his fat tongue, "I could do with a snack, myself. Bar-durp."

Polly returned to the dining-room with the frog hopping happily behind her. At first, her stepmother looked angry, and then a wicked smile slithered across her face. This was the perfect opportunity to make fun of her pretty stepdaughter.

"Oh, I see you've found a new friend?" she sneered. "He seems a perfect match for you."

"Bar-durp," said the frog. "It's very hard to see down here. Could I hop onto your lap?"

What could Polly do? She had promised. So she picked the frog up (he was very slimy!) and put him on her lap.

The stepmother laughed. She giggled. She guffawed. This was very funny indeed.

Then the frog made his next request.

"Your food smells very good. Bar-durp. Do you think I could have a bite?"

The stepmother was howling now. "Yes, yes!" she laughed. "Let's see you feed your little froggy friend!"

Polly sighed and shook her head. Then she scooped up a bit of her dinner and fed it to the frog.

"MMMM," said the frog. "Delicious. Bar-durp."

"Perhaps the froggy would like a drink, as well," the stepmother teased.

"No, thank you," the frog croaked. "But I do have one more request. I wonder if Polly would kiss me – right here on the cheek!"

The stepmother coughed, then choked, then shrieked with laughter.

Polly turned bright red.

"I thought you were my friend," she whispered to the frog.

"I am. Bar-durp. Trust me – friends keep their promises."

"So they do," sighed Polly. And she shut her eyes and kissed the frog on his green, slimy cheek…

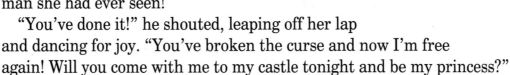

But when Polly opened her eyes, the frog was gone! And in his place sat the most handsome young man she had ever seen!

"You've done it!" he shouted, leaping off her lap and dancing for joy. "You've broken the curse and now I'm free again! Will you come with me to my castle tonight and be my princess?"

Polly looked at her father and her stepmother. Her father looked amazed and the wicked stepmother was no longer laughing.

"Yes," she said at last. "Yes, I will. I think I would like that very much. But what about them?"

"Well," said the prince, as he stared at the stepmother, "we do have a great many wells and a kitchen full of sieves. I suppose we could use the help."

"No, please don't worry," the stepmother muttered. "We'll stay right here."

"Yes," her father agreed. "You two young people go off and enjoy yourselves."

And so they did. Polly married the prince. They went to live in his castle. And the girl who kept her promise to a fat, friendly frog lived happily after after. Bar-durp.

Rabbit and Tiger Go Fishing

It was late, very late, and Rabbit sat by the side of the river, fishing. A night breeze blew. The river rippled gently by. And the moon shone in the water like a bright, yellow ball.

Suddenly, Tiger burst through the jungle leaves and breathed hot and heavy down Rabbit's back!

"I've got you now!" he growled. "There is no way you can escape."

Rabbit trembled. Perhaps this time Tiger was right. And then he saw the moon's reflection in the water, and he had an idea.

"Oh dear," he muttered, "you've come at a very bad time, Tiger. Do you see that cheese in the water, there? I was just about to pull it up from the bottom." And he pointed at the reflection of the moon!

Now if there was anything that Tiger liked to eat more than rabbit, it was cheese.

"Let me have that!" he growled again. And he snatched the fishing-rod from Rabbit's paws. But when he pulled up the line, there was nothing on it.

"See what you've done!" Rabbit scolded. "In your hurry, you let the cheese get away. But I can still see it down there. Perhaps if you were to dive in and grab it with your strong claws…

"Excellent!" Tiger roared. "And when I return I shall have rabbit and cheese for supper tonight!"

So into the water he jumped. And, as soon as Tiger went "SPLASH!", Rabbit scampered home.

He got free.

He got safe.

He got clean away.

And all Tiger got was… wet.

The Mouse Deer's Wisdom

Once there lived a baker – a fat and wealthy baker – who baked the best cakes in the land. But this baker – this fat and wealthy baker – had a problem. So he went to see the king.

"Your Majesty," the baker explained, "I have a problem. Next to my bakery, there is a little house. And in that little house there lives a little family – a mother, a father and two small children. They are poor, to be sure, but for many years now, day after day, they have freely enjoyed the privilege of smelling my wonderful cakes. Do you not think that they owe me just a little money for that pleasure?"

The king stroked his beard and thought. This was a difficult question, indeed. So he called his wise men and his magicians and his advisers and shared the problem with them. And soon they were stroking their beards too. No one had an answer.

"I know what we must do," the king said finally, "we must send for the Mouse Deer!"

The Mouse Deer – who lived in the jungle near the king's palace – was by far the wisest creature in the land.

He had to be, you see, for he was also one of the smallest and would have been eaten up long ago were it not for his wisdom and wit.

One of the king's advisers was sent to fetch the Mouse Deer and tell him the baker's problem.

The Mouse Deer came at once. He bowed to the king. Then he grinned a sly grin, and said, "Your Majesty, I have considered the baker's problem with great care. And now I have an answer: the baker must be paid!"

The surprised advisers looked at each other. But the baker could only smile.

"What is more," the Mouse Deer continued, "because even the smell of his wonderful cakes is a pleasure fit for a king, the baker must be paid a king's reward – a thousand gold pieces!"

The astonished advisers' jaws dropped. But it was all the baker could do to keep from dancing. "Sadly," the Mouse Deer concluded, "this poor family cannot afford such a great sum. So I shall pay the baker myself – right here in court – if Your Majesty would be so kind as to lend me the money."

The king stroked his beard again. He did not know what the little animal was up to, but he trusted him. So he told his treasurer to fetch a thousand gold pieces.

When the big bag of coins arrived, the Mouse Deer asked everyone to be seated.

"We need to sure it's all here," he said. And the Mouse Deer began to count.

"One gold piece," he counted. Then he threw it on the marble floor so it rang like a little gold bell.

"Two gold pieces," he counted. And that one rang against the floor as well.

"Three, four, five gold pieces," he went on, throwing each one to the floor. And so he continued, all the way to a thousand, until the whole room rang with the jingling and the jangling of the coins.

When the Mouse Deer had finally finished, the baker jumped out of his seat, eager to scoop up his treasure. But before he could pick up even one piece, the Mouse Deer raised a tiny hoof.

"Wait just a minute," he said. "There is no need for you to pick up these coins, for you have been paid already!"

The baker stopped and stared.

The king scratched his head.

The advisers all said, "Huh?"

And so the Mouse Deer explained, "You say that poor family owed you money for the pleasure of smelling your cakes, even though they never got to taste a single crumb. I say that I have paid you in the very same way. For, although you will never be able to spend even one of these gold coins, you have had the pleasure of hearing them being counted. Hearing the coins for smelling the cakes – it seems a fair trade to me."

The baker turned to the king in anger, but all the king could do was smile.

"It seems a fair trade to me, as well," he said. Then, without a smile, he added, "From now on, that poor family could do with less of your greed and more of your kindness."

The baker lowered his head and bowed. Then he slipped sheepishly out of the palace, never to return.

The advisers applauded, the magicians marvelled, and the wise men cheered, "Hooray!"

And the Mouse Deer returned to his home in the jungle, still the wisest creature in all the land!

The Four Friends

It was evening. The long, hot day was over. And the four friends gathered by the water-hole.

"Good evening to you all," called Raven, high in the branches of a tree.

"I hope everyone is well," chirped Rat, as he crawled out of his hole in the muddy bank.

"Very well, indeed," yawned Turtle, as he floated lazily to the water's surface.

"And very happy to be among friends," added Goat, as she bent down to take a drink.

The four friends talked and laughed and played by the water's edge. Then they went their separate ways for the night, promising to return the next evening.

But when the next evening came, someone was missing.

"Greetings, one and all," called Raven, high in the branches of a tree.

"And how is everyone tonight?" chirped Rat, as he crawled out of his hole in the muddy bank.

"Very well, indeed," yawned Turtle, as he floated lazily to the water's surface. But when it was time for Goat to speak, Goat was not there!

"Perhaps she's late," called Raven, flying down to join the others.

"Perhaps she's with her family," suggested Rat, pacing back and forth in front of his hole.

"Perhaps she's met the Hunter!" cried Turtle, as he pulled his worried face deep into his shell.

"Well, if that's the case," said Raven, "I must go and look for her. We're four friends, right? And we have promised always to help each other."

So off Raven flew, high above the jungle.

He looked left and he looked right.

He looked high and he looked low.

And finally he found what he was looking for – his friend Goat, trapped in the Hunter's net.

"Help me. Please help me!" Goat cried. "The Hunter has gone off to check his other nets, but when he returns he will kill me."

Faster than he had ever flown before, Raven darted back to the water-hole.

"This may hurt a little," he explained to Rat. "I am going to pick you up

39

with my claws and carry you to Goat. She is trapped in the Hunter's net and only your sharp teeth can set her free."

So Raven grabbed Rat with his sharp claws and carried him over the trees to Goat.

Rat had never been so frightened. But when he saw his poor friend, he forgot all about his fear, and set to gnawing through the net.

Turtle, meanwhile, swam back and forth impatiently across the water-hole.

"My friend is in trouble," he muttered to himself, "and I must do what I can to help."

So he climbed out of the water-hole and trundled slowly across the jungle floor, in the direction that Raven had flown.

"Hurry!" cried Raven, watching carefully for the Hunter's return. "He could be back any minute!"

"I'm chewing as fast as I can," mumbled Rat through a mouthful of net. "But these ropes are strong."

Raven watched.

Rat chewed.

Goat strained against the net and finally, with a SNAP, she was free!

Just then, there came a rustling noise from the bushes behind them. The three friends froze with fear!

"Hello, everyone," puffed Turtle, breathlessly. "What can I do to help?"

"Turtle!" cried Raven. "What are you doing here?"

"We've already set Goat free," Rat explained. "And now it's time for us to run."

"But you are so slow," moaned Goat. "However will you get away?"

"We'll find out soon enough," announced Raven, "for here comes the Hunter!"

The Hunter burst through the undergrowth, and the four friends set off in all directions. Raven took to the air. Rat scurried under a log. Goat raced off across the jungle. But all poor Turtle could do was pull in his legs and hope that the Hunter would not see him.

The Hunter, however, had far better eyesight than that.

"The goat is gone!" he sighed. "But never mind, here is a nice fat turtle, just right for my dinner." And he picked up Turtle and dropped him into his hunter's sack.

Raven watched it all, and flew off to fetch Goat. He whispered a plan in her ear and, even before he had finished, she agreed, "I'll do it!"

Then, instead of running even farther away from the Hunter, she ran right towards him. He spotted her at once, and the chase began.

Goat was too fast for him. Far too fast. The Hunter threw down his big stick. He threw off his coat. And at last he threw down the sack that held Turtle – all to gain more speed.

"I'll be back for you later!" he shouted. And he hurried after Goat, who led him far away from Turtle before making her escape.

Meanwhile Raven found Rat, and the two of them chopped and chewed away at the sack until there was a hole big enough for Turtle to wriggle out.

The next evening, the four friends gathered, as usual, at the water-hole.

"Good evening to you all!" called Raven, high in the branches of a tree.

"And how is everyone," chirped Rat, "after our great adventure?"

"Very well indeed," yawned Turtle. "Happy to be alive!"

"And happier than ever," added Goat, "to be among friends!"

41

The Brave Bull Calf

Once upon a time, there lived a boy – a boy who owned a baby bull. They raced and they wrestled. They butted and they kicked. They did everything together. They were the very best of friends.

But the boy grew. And the baby bull did too. Until, one day, the boy's wicked stepfather announced that it was time to take the bull to market.

The boy was horrified. And so, that very night, he set off with the bull – to save his friend's life and to seek his fortune.

They walked for a night and a day, through forests and towns and fields. And, at the end of the day, the boy begged a loaf of bread from a friendly old farmer.

"Here you go," he said to the bull. "Half for you and half for me."

"You have it all," the bull snorted. "I am happy just to chew on a little grass."

"Oh no," said the boy. "We are friends, and always will be. And friends share whatever they have."

The next day was much the same. They walked through fields and towns and forests. And at the end of the day, they begged a chunk of cheese from a tired little tinker.

"Here you go," said the boy to the bull. "Half for you and half for me."

"You have it all," the bull said again. "I am happy just to munch on a bit of clover."

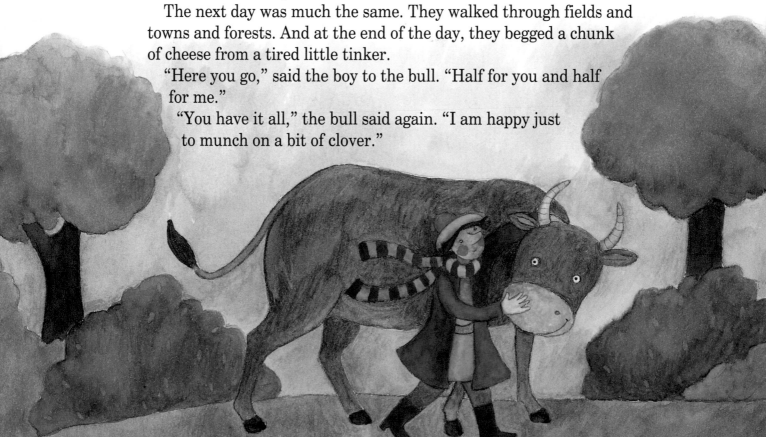

"Oh no," the boy said. "We are friends, and always will be. And friends share whatever they have."

On the third day, they walked farther still, through fields and forests and towns. And at the end of the day, they begged a fresh turnip from a short, stout shopkeeper.

"Here you go," said the boy again. "Half for you and half for me."

But this time the bull said nothing.

"What's the matter?" asked the boy. "You've been quiet all day long."

"I had a dream last night," whispered the bull. "A sad and scary dream. Tomorrow we will not walk through forests and fields and towns. We will wander into the wild woods. We will meet a tiger, a leopard, and a dragon. I will fight the first two and defeat them. And then I will fight the dragon – and he will kill me."

"No!" cried the boy, wrapping his arms around the bull's neck. "That will not happen! I won't let it!"

"But you must," said the bull. "For that is the only way you will find your fortune. When I am dead, you must cut off my right horn. It will be more powerful than ever, then. And you can use it to kill the dragon."

"No!" said the boy. "I won't!"

"But you must," said the bull again. "For you are my friend, and always will be. And friends share whatever they have."

Neither the boy nor the bull slept well that night. And the next morning they walked, step by sorry step, towards the wild woods.

"This is the place," said the bull, at last. "The place I saw in my dream. Now climb this tree. Climb high and hide yourself. And I will do my best to protect you."

The boy had hardly reached the top, when the tiger appeared, eyes flashing and sharp teeth bared.

The bull snorted. The tiger roared. And soon they were fighting for their lives. But the bull's huge horns and sharp hooves proved too much for the tiger, and before long, he limped away into the woods.

The bull hardly had time to lick his wounds when the leopard appeared. The bull bellowed. The leopard growled. But he was no match for the bull, '*her. He spat and he clawed and he bit. But in the end he crept away, ⁻ᵈ bruised, just like the tiger.

ᵘᵗ to holler, "Hooray!" when he felt the tree shake ⁻ᵗ the tree, but the ground as well. And that's when ᵠaming, tail slashing, as tall as a tree himself!

The bull snorted and pawed and rushed at the monster, but it was no use. The dragon raised its long neck, lashed out with its giant claw, and the poor bull fell to the ground. Fell to rise no more.

The dragon shook its scaly head and roared, then lumbered away into the woods. And when he had gone, the boy climbed down from the tree and wept over his dead friend.

"I will not forget you," he vowed, as he cut off the bull's right horn. "I will use this horn, just as you said. I promise to make you proud of me."

With the horn tucked in his belt, the boy set off through the wild woods. He walked sadly. He walked carefully, ready to fight off any enemy he might find. But all he found was a girl – a beautiful girl – tied to an old oak tree.

"Help me!" the girl cried. "Please help me! My father, the king, has left me here to be eaten by the dragon. He says it's the only way to stop the monster attacking our town."

The boy was sorry for the princess, but just as he was untying her he felt the ground shake once more. And, with a flash of his tail and a fiery roar, the dragon appeared! The princess screamed. The boy wanted to scream, too. And to run away as far as he could. But he remembered his friend's dream, and what his friend had died for. So he ran straight at the dragon, as fast as he could.

Just as the dragon reached out to maul him,
he drove the point of the bull's horn into the
soft sole of the dragon's foot, and the dragon
fell down dead!

The boy pulled the horn out of the dragon's foot, and then finished
untying the princess.

"What's going on here?" came a deep voice from the woods. It was the
king.

"I ordered you to stay here!" the king said to the princess. "To save our
people from the dragon."

"But Father," the girl explained, "this boy has already done that. He has
killed the dragon and saved our people – me as well!"

"Excellent!" shouted the king. "Then he must have a reward.
What say we give him your hand in marriage? And my throne when
I am gone?"

The boy looked at the princess. The princess looked at the boy.
It seemed a good idea to both of them – so they were married.
And when the time came for him to be king, he ordered
a new coat of arms decorated with a tree in one
corner, a fallen dragon on the other – and,
in the middle, the head of a bull with
one horn.

Tiger Gets Stuck

One day, quite by accident, Tiger stumbled across Rabbit's hidey-hole.

He wanted to roar for joy, but decided instead to keep very quiet, and watch and wait for Rabbit to leave.

When, at last, Rabbit hopped away into the jungle, Tiger bounded over to the hole and peered down inside. He knew exactly what he wanted to do.

Tiger slipped one front paw down into the hole. And then he slipped in the other. Next he squeezed his head in, and his shoulders, and his long, striped body. Finally he pulled in his powerful back legs. And he grinned.

"I will wait in here," Tiger chuckled. "I will wait very quietly. And when Rabbit comes home, I will gobble him up!"

Unfortunately Tiger had forgotten something. Something that Rabbit saw the minute he got close to home. Tiger forgot that his tail was still sticking out of the hole – waving a warning like a black-and-orange striped flag!

"Hmmm," thought Rabbit. "It looks as if I have a visitor."

And so he called, "Hey, Hidey-hole! Ho, Hidey-hole! Are you happy, Hidey-hole?"

Tiger (who still had no idea where his tail was) looked worried.

"Rabbit is talking to his hidey-hole," he thought. "I must keep very quiet indeed."

But just then, Rabbit called again, "Hey, Hidey-hole! Ho, Hidey-hole! Are you happy, Hidey-hole?"

"Oh dear," thought Tiger. "What if Rabbit suspects something is wrong? Perhaps I should answer, after all."

So the next time Rabbit called, "Hey Hidey-hole! Ho, Hidey-hole! Are you happy, Hidey-hole?", Tiger called back, "Yes, Mr Rabbit, I am very happy, indeed!"

But he said it in such a ridiculous, squeaky little voice that Rabbit could not keep from laughing.

"You silly Tiger," he called. "Hidey-holes don't talk! And they don't have long, striped tails sticking out of them either! It looks as if I've tricked you again."

"Oh no, you haven't," Tiger growled, "for now I will come out and eat you!"

But the minute Tiger tried to back himself out of the hidey-hole, he discovered that he was stuck! He scrunched and stretched and squeezed. He wrestled and wriggled and roared. But no amount of moving could get him out.

"Wait right there," chuckled Rabbit, "and I will fetch some help. That is, if you promise never to visit my home again."

"I do," Tiger whined, for he very much wanted to get out.

So Rabbit fetched Crocodile. And Crocodile clamped his sharp teeth round Tiger's tail. And, after much huffing and puffing and pulling, Tiger came out with a "pop!" and ran off, embarrassed, into the jungle.

Tiger kept his promise and never came back to Rabbit's home.

And Rabbit never again went home without asking his hidey-hole if it was happy or not.

The Clever Mouse

Many years ago, in a little Welsh town, there was a famine. There was no food anywhere. And everyone – from the richest lord to the poorest peasant – was tired and thin and hungry.

One day, a monk named Cadog came to visit the town. Cadog was good and gentle and kind. He loved God. He loved God's creatures. And he loved to read and write and learn. In fact, that was why he had come to the town – to study under a wise and famous teacher.

"You may be my student," the teacher promised, "but I must warn you. There is a famine in these parts, so I have nothing to feed you."

Cadog didn't mind. Not one bit. He studied hard, day after day at his little desk. And every day he had a visitor – a tiny visitor with fine, grey whiskers, a pointed nose, and a long, pink tail. He climbed on Cadog's desk, and scurried across his books, and scampered over his pile of goose-quill pens.

But Cadog didn't mind. Not one bit. He liked the little mouse and refused to chase him away. And perhaps that is why, one day, the little mouse arrived with a gift.

He climbed onto Cadog's desk. He scampered over Cadog's pens. And, in the middle of Cadog's book, he dropped one yellow grain of wheat!

"Thank you, my friend," said Cadog to the mouse.

And the mouse sat up and squeaked, as if to say, "You're welcome."

Half an hour later he returned with another piece of wheat and Cadog thanked him again.

Soon, the mouse returned a third time. Then a fourth. And a fifth. And a sixth. And when there were finally seven golden grains of wheat lying on his book, Cadog had an idea.

He took a long piece of silken thread and gently tied one end around the mouse's leg.

"This won't hurt at all," he promised. "And it may do a world of good." Then he let the mouse go and watched to see where it would run. The mouse was much too fast for Cadog, of course, but by following the silken thread he was able to trace the mouse's path – into a hole in the wall, out the other side, across the garden, through the woods, and into a huge earthen mound.

Cadog ran to fetch his teacher, and together they dug into the mound. Buried deep within were the ruins of an old house. And buried deep in the cellar of that old house was an enormous pile of wheat!

Cadog and his teacher ran to tell their friends. And soon the town was filled with the smell of freshly baked bread. Now there was plenty of food for everyone!

The next day, the little mouse came to visit, as usual. He climbed onto Cadog's desk. He scampered over Cadog's pens. And when he sat down in the middle of Cadog's book, the monk gently untied the silken thread.

"Thank you, my friend," he said. "God sent you to me for a reason. And now we know what it was. Your keen nose and tiny feet have saved the entire town."

Then he tore off a chunk of fresh, warm bread, and set it before the little creature. And the mouse and the monk shared a meal together.

The Amazing Pine Cone

When the old man wandered into town, no one paid attention. He tipped his tattered cap. He waved his wrinkled hand. But everyone ignored him, for he looked just like a beggar.

When the old man wandered through town, he tottered up the hill to the mayor's house. The house was big and bright and beautiful. It was the finest house in town by far. The old man raised his gnarled cane and rapped on the front door.

"What do you want?" called the mayor's wife, as she eased the door open and peered through the gap.

"A place to stay," the man replied, "to rest for just one night."

The mayor's wife looked at the old man. She looked at his tattered cap. She looked at his shabby coat. And she quickly shut the door.

"Go away!" she shouted. "We have no room for beggars here!"

The old man wandered back through town. He tipped his tattered cap. He waved his wrinkled hand. And still no on paid any attention. He came, at last, to another house – a poor, pathetic, little place. And he rapped on the door with his cane.

A poor, little woman answered the door. And when she saw the old man and his beggar's clothes, she felt sorry for him.

"How can I help you?" she asked.

"I need a place to stay," said the old man again, "to rest for just one night."

"Of course!" she smiled. And she welcomed him into her home.

Next morning, the old man

rose early, but before he said goodbye, he reached into his pocket with his wrinkled hand.

"I want to give you something," he said to the woman. "It is my way of saying thank you."

And he handed the woman a pine cone!

The woman didn't know what to say. No one had ever given her a pine cone before. So she smiled as politely as she could, and tried very hard not to giggle.

"This is no ordinary pine cone," the old man explained. "It is a magic pine cone. And it will multiply by a thousand times the first thing you do today!"

The woman smiled again. She liked the old man. She appreciated his kindness. But this was the strangest thing she had ever heard.

She said goodbye, and when the old man had gone, she turned to a piece of cloth she had woven the night before. She pulled it out of the basket to fold it, but the more she pulled out and the more she folded, the more cloth there was! Soon, not only her living-room, but her kitchen and her bedroom and the whole of the house was filled with brand new cloth.

The woman shook her head, amazed. So it really was a magic pine cone after all! And it wasn't long before the whole town learned of the woman's good fortune and the old man's magical gift.

Exactly one year later, the old man wandered into the town again. This time no one ignored him. He tipped his tattered cap. He waved his wrinkled hand. And everyone stopped and smiled and invited him to spend the night.

But, just as he had done before, he wandered through the town to the top of the hill, and knocked on the mayor's door.

The mayor's wife welcomed him with open arms. She gave him the nicest room and the most comfortable bed, and she cooked him a delicious meal.

51

And as soon as he had gone to bed, she put a pile of gold coins on the table, ready to be counted the moment she received his thank you gift.

Next morning, just as she had expected, the old man reached into his pocket and handed her a pine cone.

"This is no ordinary pine cone," he explained. "It is a magic pine cone. And it will multiply by a thousand times the first thing you do today."

The mayor's wife nodded and smiled. She could hardly wait for the old man to go. And, as soon as she had shut the door behind him, she raced to the table, ready to count her gold. But before she got there, something happened. Something she had not expected.

The mayor's wife sneezed. And because that was the first thing she did, she sneezed not one, not twice, but a thousand times – for the rest of that day, and the next, and the one after that!

The whole town heard of it, of course. News even reached the old man, who smiled and patted his pocketful of pine cones, and then wandered off to another town, tipping his tattered cap, waving his wrinkled hand, and looking for somewhere to spend the night.

The Very Strong Sparrow

"Too-tweet! Too-tweet! Too-tweet!" the baby birds cried out for their mother.

"Patience, patience," said Sparrow. "I've got food enough for everyone here." And she fed them and hugged them, then wrapped her wings around them. And soon they were fast asleep.

KA-THOOM! KA-THOOM! KA-THOOM!

Elephant came tramping through the jungle. The earth shook, the trees shook. And so did poor Sparrow's nest.

"Too-tweet! Too-tweet! Too-tweet!" cried the baby birds. They were startled, and frightened, and wide awake!

Sparrow was furious. "See what you've done!" she complained to Elephant. "You woke up my babies with your tramping and your tromping and your trumpeting. Could you try to be a little quieter?"

KA-THOOM! KA-THOOM! KA-THOOM!

Elephant tramped over to Sparrow's tree.

"Who do you think you're talking to?" he demanded. "You are nothing but a tiny little sparrow. I am Elephant – the strongest animal in the jungle. And I will do whatever I please."

"The strongest animal in the jungle? I don't believe it," said Sparrow. And then, without thinking, she added, "Why, even I could beat a big bully like you."

Elephant tossed his trunk in the air and gave a trumpet blast. He had never been so insulted. "Meet me tomorrow at noon, at the old banana tree," he roared. "We will have a test of strength and see who is the strongest animal in the jungle." Then he tramped away, angry: KA-THOOM! KA-THOOM! KA-THOOM!

"What have I done?" thought Sparrow. "Well, I had to do something. He was waking up my babies, after all."

Later that day, Sparrow flew to the river, to take a bath and to fetch some water for her children. But just as she landed at the water's edge, Crocodile appeared.

KER-SPLASH! KER-SPLASH! KER-SPLASH!

He thrashed his scaly tail back and forth across the water till Sparrow thought she was going to drown.

"Stop it!" she cried. "All I want is a little water for myself and my babies."

53

"Who do you think you are talking to?" snapped Crocodile. "You are nothing but a tiny little sparrow. And I am Crocodile – the strongest animal in the jungle. And I will do whatever I please."

Sparrow had heard this before, and she was about to fly away, when she had an idea.

"The strongest animal in the jungle?" she laughed. "I don't believe it. I will meet you here, tomorrow, just after noon. And I will show you that I am more powerful than you can every hope to be."

Crocodile laughed so hard, there were tears in his eyes.

"I'll take you up on that," he chuckled. "And if you win, you may drink from my river whenever you like."

The next day, as the sun reached the top of the sky, Sparrow met Elephant by the old banana tree. She had the end of a long, thick vine in her beak.

"For our test of strength," she said, "we shall have a tug of war. You hold this end of the vine, and I will fly off and grab hold of the other end. And when I cry 'Pull!' we shall see who is the strongest."

KA-THOOM! KA-THOOM! KA-THOOM!

Elephant tramped up and down with joy. He could win this contest easily! So he took the vine from Sparrow and she flew off to grab the other end.

But when she picked up the other end, she did not cry "Pull!". At least, not straightaway. No, she carried the vine to the river, where Crocodile was waiting.

KER-SPLASH! KER-SPLASH! KER-SPLASH!

"So you've come after all," he sneered.

"Yes," she said. "And I've come to win! We shall have a tug of war. You take this end, and I will fly off and grab the other end. And when I cry 'Pull!' we shall see who is the strongest."

Crocodile chuckled and clamped his teeth onto the end of the vine. Then Sparrow flew to the middle of the vine – to a spot where she could hear both Elephant and Crocodile, but where they could not hear each other. And that's when she cried, "PULL!"

KA-THOOM! KA-THOOM! KA-THOOM!

Elephant pulled – feet stomping, neck straining, trunk swinging up and down.

KER-SPLASH! KER-SPLASH! KER-SPLASH!

Crocodile pulled as well – feet splashing, teeth gnashing, tail thrashing back and forth.

They pulled for an hour. They pulled for two. But, pull as they might, neither could budge the other. At last, Elephant called through his aching teeth, "Sparrow, I give up! I never would have believed it, but you are every bit as strong as I am. From now on I will tiptoe quietly past your tree."

Crocodile called out, as well. "You win, mighty Sparrow. From now on, you may drink from my river whenever you like."

So Sparrow went home to her little nest. And when she told her babies what she had done, they laughed and clapped their wings and cheered, "Too-tweet! Too-tweet! Too-tweet!" For their mother was now the strongest animal in the jungle!

Simple John

Once upon a time, there were three brothers who went off to seek their fortune.

The two older brothers were very clever. But the third brother was not clever at all. His name was John, and the two older brothers were not very nice to him. They made fun of him, and picked on him, and called him names like "simple" and "stupid" and "fool".

On the first day, they came across a huge mound of earth, tall and thin and teeming with ants.

"Ants are nasty!" shuddered the eldest brother.

"And they're good for nothing but treading on," said the second brother.

But just as the two older brothers went to knock the anthill down, the third brother, John, stepped in their way.

"No!" he shouted. "Ants are nice. They are black and tiny and creepy and crawly. And they're fun to watch. It wouldn't be kind to knock their house down."

The older brothers looked at each other and shook their heads.

"Not very clever," one whispered.

"Doesn't know a thing about insects," whispered the other one.

But in the end they grew tired of arguing and agreed to leave the ants alone.

The next day, the three brothers came across a pond full of ducks.

"Ducks are tasty!" said the oldest brother.

"Ducks are delicious!" drooled the second brother.

But, just as the clever brothers aimed their arrows at the ducks, the third brother, John, stepped in their way.

"No!" he shouted. "Ducks are nice. They have flappy wings and webby feet and quacky voices. It wouldn't be kind to kill them."

The older brothers looked in the air and sighed.

"Doesn't know a thing about ducks," one whispered.

"Nor good eating, neither," whispered the other one.

But in the end they grew tired of arguing and agreed to leave the ducks alone.

On the third day, the three brothers came across a bees' nest tucked in the trunk of a thick, tall tree.

"Look at the honey!" said the oldest brother.

"Now that's good eating!" said the second brother.

But, just as the clever brothers were about to light a fire and smoke the bees out of the tree, the third brother, John, stepped in their way.

"No!" he shouted. "Bees are nice. They are yellow and stripy and sticky and buzzy. It wouldn't be kind to steal their honey."

The clever brothers crossed their arms and scowled.

"He's starting to get on my nerves," whispered one.

"Mine, too," whispered the other one.

But in the end they grew tired of arguing and agreed to leave the bees alone.

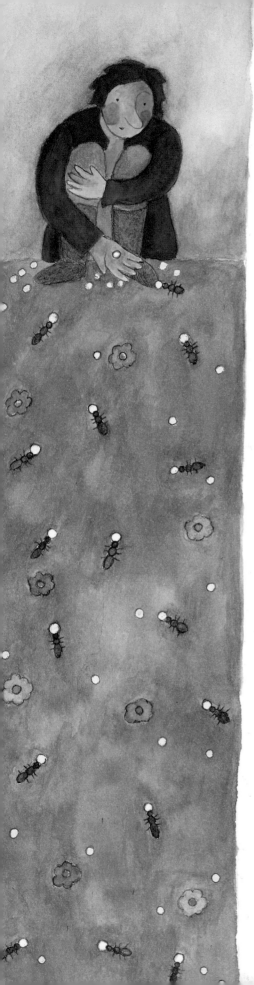

Later that day, the three brothers came to a castle. A castle with stone walls and stone towers and, standing inside, stone statue horses and peasants and princes. Indeed, the only thing that was not stone was a little bearded man who came to greet them.

"Thank you for coming," he said. "Thank you very much! We shall have some supper and get a good night's rest. Then tomorrow you must try to break the spell that has turned this castle to stone – and win for yourselves a great fortune!"

The brothers didn't know about breaking spells, but they were hungry and tired, and so they accepted the little man's invitation. They ate like horses and slept like logs. And, in the morning, it was the eldest brother who chose to go first.

"To break the spell," explained the little man, "you must perform three tasks. Before she was turned to stone, our Queen broke a necklace in the forest, and a thousand pearls were scattered across the ground. The first task is to gather up those pearls before sunset – or you, too, will be turned to stone."

The eldest brother went out into the forest to look for the pearls. They were everywhere! Under rocks and ferns and fallen leaves. But, clever as he was, he only managed to collect a hundred before the sun set. So he was turned to stone.

The next day, the second brother went to the forest. And, even though he managed to collect two hundred pearls, at the setting of the sun he too was turned to stone.

"What chance do I have?" thought John, as he set off on the third day. "I'm not clever at all!" And then he heard a sound in the grass below.

"Hello, John!" called a tiny voice. "I am the King of the Ants. You saved our anthill, and now we would like to help you. All my people are here – thousands of them! – and we will find the pearls for you."

And so they did – every last one!

"Excellent!" said the little man. "For your second task, you must find a silver key, which the Queen dropped in the lake."

Again, poor John didn't know what to do. But just then, a big, brown duck flew overhead. "Don't worry, John," the duck called. "You helped us and now we will help you."

And with that, a whole flight of ducks plunged beneath the water, and came up again with the silver key.

"One more task," the little man said, excited now. "But we must hurry, for the sun is setting fast. The King has three daughters, who all look alike. But the one he loves the most was eating a little honey cake just before she was turned to stone. You must find her and kiss her."

"No problem at all," buzzed a voice in John"s ear. "I am the Queen Bee. And because you would not steal from us, I will help you find the princess." The Queen Bee sniffed and sniffed at the lips of every stone girl in the castle, and finally she found one that smelled of honey.

John pursed his lips and kissed the stone statue, and immediately everything that had been turned to stone – including his brothers – became flesh and blood again!

And what was John's reward? He married the girl that he kissed. And his brothers married her sisters. And that is how the three brothers found their fortune – with the help of the least clever brother of them all.

The Selfish Sand Frog

Sand Frog was thirsty. So he went to the water-hole to have a drink. He drank and he drank and he drank. And the more he drank, the bigger he grew. He drank so much, in fact, that he drank that water-hole dry!

Dingo, Goanna, and Kangaroo complained. "Hey, Sand Frog," they cried, "don't be so greedy. We need water, too!"

But Sand Frog ignored them. He was still thirsty, you see. So he hopped away to find more water.

Soon he came to a billabong. He drank and he drank and he drank. And the more he drank, the bigger he grew. He drank so much, in fact, that he drank that little swamp dry!

The newts and the tortoises and the tadpoles complained. "Hey Sand Frog," they cried, "don't be so greedy. We need water, too!"

But Sand Frog ignored them. He was still thirsty, you see. So he hopped away to find more water.

Soon he came to a lake. And you can guess what happened. He drank and he drank and he drank. And the more he drank, the bigger he grew. He drank so much, in fact, that he drank that lake dry!

The fish flipped and flopped around on the pebbly bottom. "Hey Sand Frog," they complained, "don't be so greedy. We need water, too!"

But Sand Frog ignored them. He was still thirsty, you see. So he hopped away to find more water.

60

Rivers and lakes and streams.

Swamps and ponds and creeks.

Sand Frog drank the water from them all – until there was no water left anywhere! And, by that time, he was so enormous that the only place he could find to sit was on the top of a great mountain.

The other animals were angry. So they grabbed their spears and set off to find him. Eagle saw him first, and he led the others to the mountain where Sand Frog sat.

"Give us our water back!" the animals cried. But, once again, Sand Frog ignored them. He wasn't thirsty any more. He was full. He was happy. And he was bigger than any of them.

One by one, the animals threw their sharp spears at Sand Frog.

Koala and Dingo and Bandicoot.

Platypus, Emu and Bat.

But each of them missed. Finally Kangaroo aimed his long spear and threw it. He struck Sand Frog in the side, and the water gushed out of him, down the mountain, and back into the rivers and lakes and streams!

The other animals cheered. They drank and swam and splashed about.

But Sand Frog hopped sadly and painfully home. He was little again, and ashamed for having been so greedy. In fact, he dared not show his face to the other animals.

And that is why, even now, sand frogs hide in the sand all day, and only come out to play in the ponds at night.

The Mouse's Bride

It was an unusual family. An old man. An old woman. And a little mouse boy.

He was their dream-come-true. The old man and the old woman had no children of their own, but one day a hawk, soaring overhead, dropped the little mouse into the old woman's laundry basket. And from that moment on, the old man and she had raised him as their son.

The little mouse grew – as children do. And soon he was no longer a little mouse boy, but a full-grown mouse man. And he wanted more than anything to find a wife.

"I will help you, my son," said the old man. So, one warm night they set off to find the mouse a bride. The old woman waved them goodbye and wiped the tears from her eyes, for she feared that she might never see her son again.

They walked and they walked and they walked, their path lit brightly by the light of the full moon. The moon watched, and grew curious, and at last she asked, "What are you looking for?"

"A wife for my son," the old man explained.

"I see," said the moon. "Well, I would make a very good wife. I am bright and beautiful and round! Would your son agree to marry me?"

62

The mouse looked at the moon and shook his little head.

"I'm sorry," he said. "You are indeed bright and beautiful and round. But you are also cold and distant. No, you are not the wife for me."

So they walked and they walked and they walked some more, under the shadow of a dark night cloud. The cloud watched, and grew curious, and at last she asked, "What are you looking for?"

"A wife for my son," the old man explained.

"Ah," said the cloud. "Well, I would make an excellent wife. I am fluffy and puffy and soft!"

"Yes," agreed the little mouse. "But I have watched you, and you can also be angry and gloomy and very bad-tempered. No," he said, shaking his head again, "you are not the wife for me."

On they walked, far into the night now, and the wind whistled around them, and watched, and grew curious, and asked at last, "What are you looking for?"

"A wife for my son," said the old man again.

"Then look no further," said the wind. "For I would make the perfect wife. I can be both gentle and strong."

"That is just the problem," said the little mouse. "You are one way and then another, and no one can tell which way it will be. No, you are not the wife for me."

The old man and the mouse carried on a little further and, just as the old man was wondering if his son would ever find a wife, they came to a mountain.

"Ah!" said the mouse when he saw the mountain. "Now there is the wife for me. She is tall and proud and full of life. And I can trust her to stand strong and true, whatever happens. Mountain," he asked humbly, "would you be my wife?"

"It would be a pleasure," said the mountain. "Now tunnel deep within me and you will find my heart." The mouse began to dig. The old man helped him. And soon they came to a tunnel. And the tunnel led to a cave. And sitting in the middle of the cave was the most beautiful lady mouse that the little mouse had ever seen.

Together they went back to the old woman, who wept for joy when she saw them. Then the little mouse and the lady mouse were married. And they all lived happily ever after.

The Big Wave

The sea splashed gently against the sandy beach. The sandy beach lay white and hot before the little village. And in the little village lived four hundred people – old men and young men, mothers and grandmothers, babies and boys and girls.

Behind the village, green terraces rose like steps to a high, flat plateau. And on the plateau stood a fine old house, surrounded by rice fields.

In that house lived Hamaguchi – an old man, a rich man, owner of the rice fields and lord of the village below. With him lived his grandson – only ten years old, full of questions, and full of life.

One hot summer evening, Hamaguchi walked slowly out onto his porch. He looked at the village below, and smiled. It was harvest time, and his people were celebrating with music and dancing and bright lantern lights.

He looked at the beach beyond, cool and quiet and calm, and he smiled again.

But when Hamaguchi looked out across the sea, his smile turned suddenly to a worried frown. For there was a wave, a wave that stretched as far as he could see, tall and wild and fierce. And it was rushing towards the village below.

Hamaguchi had never seen this kind of wave. But he had heard tales about such waves from his father and his father's father. So he called his grandson and asked him to bring a flaming torch.

"Why, Grandfather?" the boy asked, innocently. "Why do you want a torch?"

"There is not time to explain," Hamaguchi answered. "We must act quickly!" And he hobbled to the fields on the left of the house and set his crops on fire.

"Grandfather!" the boy cried. "What are you doing?"

Hamaguchi looked down at the village. No one was looking up at the plateau.

"There is no time!" he barked. "Come with me." And he took the boy by the hand and set fire to the fields on the right.

The flames burst orange and yellow and white against the night, and the boy began to weep.

"Grandfather, are you mad? This is everything you own!"

But the old man said nothing. He looked down at the village, then hurried to the remaining fields and set the torch to them, as well. The sky was filled with sparks and smoke and the little boy was sobbing now.

"Please, Grandfather! Stop, Grandfather! There will be nothing left!"

Just then, a bell sounded, ringing from the temple in the village below. And soon, streaming up the terraced hill, came the villagers – young women, old women, boys and girls, fathers and grandfathers, babies on their backs and buckets in their hands. All four hundred of them – running to help put out the fire!

And, just as they reached the burning fields, the wave struck the village below.

It sounded like thunder.

It sounded like cannon fire.

It sounded like the hoof-beats of ten thousand horses.

It destroyed everything in its path, and when at last it rumbled and rolled back out to sea, there was not a single house left standing.

The people looked in horror at the ruins of their village. But when at last they turned to face the fields, they were gone as well – burned to the ground.

Hamaguchi's grandson grabbed him round the waist and, sobbing still, asked the question everyone else wanted to hear.

"Why, Grandfather? Why did you burn down your precious fields?"

"Don't you see?" the old man said to the crowd. "I had to find some way to warn you – to lead you out of harm's way. For, as precious as my fields are to me, each and every one of you is more precious still."

And with that, Hamaguchi invited them all to stay in his house until the village was rebuilt.

The old man lived many more years, but when, at last, he died, the people built a little shrine in their village, in memory of the lord who sacrificed all he had to save them from the terrible wave.

Tiger and the Storm

One evening, just as it was turning dark, Rabbit wandered out into the jungle, together with his wife and their friends, Owl and Dog.

Along the way, they spotted some fallen vines. So they stopped and gathered up the vines, hoping to weave them into a length of good, strong rope.

Suddenly, Rabbit heard something: the twitch of a tail, a long, low growl, the crush of a strong, striped paw.

"Tiger is coming," he whispered to the others. "Quick, hide behind that rock. And I will deal with him."

The others did as Rabbit said and, just a moment later, Tiger burst out of the bushes.

"Aha!" he roared. "I have you cornered once again. There is no way you can escape this time!"

"Oh dear," said Rabbit sadly. "You have such bad timing, Tiger. Haven't you heard? There is a great storm coming this way – a hurricane, I believe – and I was just tying myself to this tree so I would not be blown away. If you have any sense, I suggest you do the same."

"Nonsense!" Tiger roared. "This is just another one of your tricks. You have made a fool of me before, but I will not be fooled again!"

"All right," Rabbit sighed. "Eat me if you like. But before you have finished, the storm will blow you clear across the jungle. Listen," (and he said this in the direction of the rock) "you can hear the pitter-patter of rain even now."

Rabbit's wife was listening. So she began to thump the ground with her big back legs: pitter-patter, pitter-patter, pitter-patter.

"Oh dear," Tiger paused. "Perhaps you are right, after all. But perhaps it is nothing more than a light shower! I will eat you now. I don't mind getting wet."

"A light shower?" Rabbit said quickly. "Then how is it that I hear the wind blowing up into a storm?"

It was Owl's turn this time. He started to flap his big brown wings, and he called, "Hoo-hoo. Hoo hoo. Hoo-hoo."

"Oh my!" Tiger was shaking now. "I believe a storm is coming, after all. But I am sure I still have time to eat you!"

"Perhaps," nodded Rabbit. "But then who will be left to help tie you to this tree? Listen, the wind is howling even harder now. The storm is almost here!"

And now Dog joined in, howling, "A-Woo! A-Woo! A-Woo!"

"All right, then. All right," Tiger whimpered.

"Quickly, tie me to the tree. And tie me tight!"

So Rabbit did just as Tiger asked. He wrapped the vines around Tiger's striped legs and Tiger's striped belly and he tied him to the tree. And all the while, his friends kept up their thumping and their hooting and their howling.

"There you go," announced Rabbit, once Tiger was tied tightly to the tree. "That should keep you from going anywhere for a while."

"But what about you?" Tiger asked.

"Oh, don't worry about me." Rabbit chuckled. "I feel very safe, now. I think the storm has passed us by. Listen."

And suddenly, the thumping and the hooting and the howling came to an end. And Rabbit's friends came out, chuckling, from behind the rock.

"You've done it again!" Tiger roared. "You've tricked me. And you're in trouble, now!"

But when Tiger went to leap at Rabbit, he found that he could not move. No, not one inch – so tightly had Rabbit tied him to that tree!

"Let me go! Let me go – NOW!" Tiger roared.

But Rabbit just grinned.

"I don't think so," he said. "For if there is one thing more dangerous than a howling storm, it's an angry, howling Tiger!"

And with that, he and his friends disappeared into the night – safe once more.

The Knee-High Man

Knee-High Man lived by a swamp, deep in the heart of Alabama.

He lived by himself, in a tiny, run-down shack, because he was ashamed of how small he was.

"I'm tired of being little," he said to himself, one day. "I'm gonna find out how to get big!"

So he went to the biggest friend he knew. He went to see Mr Horse.

"Mr Horse!" he hollered. "Mr Horse, I want to be big, like you. Tell me what I have to do."

Mr Horse munched thoughtfully on a mouthful of oats.

"Well…" he said slowly. "I always eat lots and lots of oats. Then I run and run – about twenty miles a day. That's how I got big. Maybe that'll work for you."

"Thank you," said Knee-High Man. Then he did just what Mr Horse said.

He ate oats till his stomach hurt.

He ran and ran till his little legs hurt.

But still he grew no bigger. No, not one little bit.

So he went to see his next-biggest friend. He went to see Mr Bull.

"Mr Bull!" he hollered. "Mr Bull, I want to be big, like you. Tell me what I have to do."

Mr Bull munched patiently on a mouthful of grass.

"Well…" he grunted. "I chew up field after field of grass. Then I bellow and bellow – MOOO! – for all I'm worth. That's how I got big. Maybe that'll work for you."

"Thank you," said Knee-High Man. Then he did just what Mr Bull said.

He chewed grass till his teeth hurt. He bellowed – MOOO! – till his throat hurt.

But still he grew no bigger. No, not one little bit.

So he went to see the smartest friend he knew. He went to see Mr Hoot Owl.

"Mr Hoot Owl!" he hollered. "Mr Hoot Owl, I'm tired of being a little Knee-High Man. I want to be big! Please tell me what I have to do."

Mr Hoot Owl blinked and ruffled his feathers and turned his big head round and round.

"Hoo-hoo! Tell me, Mr Knee-High Man," he said, at last. "Why do you want to be big?"

"Because I'm tired of always looking up at everyone," moaned Knee-High Man.

Mr Hoot Owl blinked and ruffled his feathers again.

"Hoo-hoo! Size isn't everything," he said. "Can you climb a tree?"

"Of course!" answered Knee-High Man.

"Then come on up here and join me," said the owl.

Knee-High Man climbed up that tree, as fast as any squirrel. Then he sat himself down on the branch beside Mr Hoot Owl.

"Now look around," said Mr Hoot Owl. "What do you see?"

Knee-High Man looked. There was Mr Horse, running around his field. And over there was Mr Bull, bellowing for all he was worth. And neither of them looked any bigger than the biggest ant!

"When you get tired of being small," said Mr Hoot Owl, "just climb up here. You'll be the tallest thing around! And when you get tired of that, climb back down – and be satisfied with what you are."

So that's just what he did.

And he was never ashamed of being a Knee-High Man again.

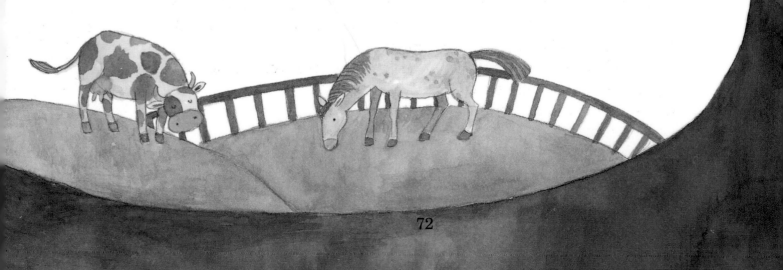

The Clever Baker

Annie was a baker – the best in all Scotland. Shortbreads and buns and cakes – she made them all. And they were so delicious that no one ever left a crumb behind, on table or plate or floor.

Now this was fine for everyone but the fairies, who depended on those crumbs, and who had never had so much as a tiny taste of one of Annie's famous cakes. So one bright morning, the Fairy King decided to do something about that. He hid himself among the wild flowers by the side of the road, and when Annie passed on her way to market, he sprinkled fairy dust in her eyes to make her fall fast asleep.

When Annie awoke, she was no longer on the road, but deep in fairyland, face to face with the Fairy King.

"Annie!" the King commanded. "Everyone has tasted your wonderful cakes. Everyone, but us! So from now on, you will stay here in fairyland and bake for us every day."

"Oh dear," thought Annie. But she didn't show that she was worried, or even scared, for she was a clever woman. No, she set her mind, at once, to making a plan for her escape.

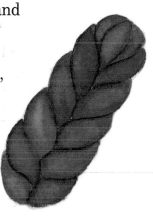

"Very well," she said. "But if I am to bake you a cake, I will need ingredients – flour and milk, eggs and sugar and butter."

"Fetch them at once!" commanded the Fairy King. So off the fairies flew, to Annie's house. And back they flew, in a flash, with everything she needed.

"Oh dear," Annie sighed, shaking her head (and still without a plan). "If I am to bake a cake, I will also need my tools – my pots and pans and pitchers and bowls and spoons."

"Fetch them, quickly!" the Fairy King commanded again. But when the fairies returned, they were in such a hurry that they stumbled and sent the pots and pans crashing and clanking across the floor.

"OOH! OWW!" cried the Fairy King, jamming his hands against his ears. "You know very well that I cannot stand loud noises!"

And, at that moment, Annie had her plan.

She broke the eggs and poured the milk and mixed in the flour and butter.

But when she stirred the batter, she made the spoon clatter – clackety, clackety, clack – against the side of the bowl.

The Fairy King winced at the noise, but Annie could see that it was not loud enough. And so she said, "Oh dear. I am used to having my little striped cat beside me when I bake. I cannot make my best cake unless he is here."

So the Fairy King commanded, and the fairies went, and came back at once with the cat.

Annie put the cat under the table and, as she mixed the batter, she trod, ever so gently, on the cat's tail.

And so the spoon went, "Clackety, clackety, clack!"

And the cat went, "Yow! Yow! Yow!"

And the Fairy King looked even more uncomfortable.

"Oh dear," said Annie again. "It's still not right. I'm also used to having my big brown dog beside me when I bake. I don't suppose...?"

"Yes, yes," sighed the Fairy King. "Anything for a taste of that cake."

And the fairies were sent for the dog.

Annie put him next to the cat, and he soon began to bark.

And so the spoon went, "Clackety, clackety, clack!"

And the cat went, "Yow! Yow! Yow!"

And the dog went, "Woof! Woof! Woof!"

And the Fairy King stuck a fairy finger in one ear.

"Just one more thing," said Annie. "I am worried about my little baby. And I cannot do my best work when I am worried."

"All right, all right," moaned the Fairy King.

And he sent off his fairies one more time.

The baby was asleep when she arrived, but as soon as she heard all the noise, she awoke with a cry.

And so the spoon went, "Clackety, clackety, clack!"

And the cat went, "Yow! Yow! Yow!"

And the dog went, "Woof! Woof! Woof!"

And the baby went, "Wah! Wah! Wah!"

And the Fairy King put his hands over his ears and shouted, "Enough! Enough! Enough!"

And everything went quiet.

"Even the best cake in the world is not worth this racket," he cried. "Take your baby, woman, and your dog and your cat and your noisy spoon. Go back to your own world, and leave us in peace!"

Annie smiled. "I'll do better than that," she said. "If you promise to leave me be, I'll put a special little cake for you and your people by the fairy mound each day."

"That's a bargain," smiled the Fairy King, and Annie and all that belonged to her were returned to her kitchen in a flash.

And every day, from then on, Annie left a little cake by the fairy mound. And the Fairy King not only left her alone; each day he left her a little bag of gold, where the cake had been. And they all lived happily ever after.

How the Kangaroo Got Its Tail

There was a time when Kangaroo had no tail. Not a bushy tail. Not a waggly tail. And certainly not the long, strong tail he has today.

Kangaroo had no tail. But what he did have were plenty of children. So many children, in fact, that some of the other animals were jealous – particularly Bandicoot, who had no children at all.

One day, Bandicoot came to visit Kangaroo.

"Kangaroo," he pleaded. "You and your wife have six beautiful children, and I have none at all. Won't you give me three of your children to raise as my own?"

Kangaroo was shocked. "No," he said, as politely as he could. "We love our children. We could never give them away."

"Two, then," begged Bandicoot. "Just let me have two. I promise to be a good father."

"No," Kangaroo insisted. "We want to raise our children ourselves, thank you very much."

"How about one, then," Bandicoot cried. "Just one, and I will never bother you again."

"No!" said Kangaroo, firmly. "We could not part with even one of our children!"

Bandicoot was angry, now. "All right," he shouted. "If you will not give me any of your children, I will have to steal one!" And he rushed towards the baby kangaroos.

"Run, children!" Kangaroo hollered. "Run away!"

The kangaroo children jumped from their mother's pouch and turned to run, but Bandicoot was too quick for them. He grabbed one of the little kangaroos from behind and held on tight.

Kangaroo was there in a second. He grabbed his child by the arms, and both he and Bandicoot began to pull.

They pulled and they pulled and they pulled. And then something strange happened.

The little kangaroo's bottom began to stretch – it grew longer and longer and longer!

"Help me, wife!" Kangaroo called. So she began to pull as well. And the little kangaroo's bottom stretched longer still.

Finally, Kangaroo called for his other children, and when they began to pull, it was too much for Bandicoot. He let go with a sigh and ran away. And the kangaroos tumbled down in a pile of pouches and feet and fur.

"Is everyone all right?" asked Kangaroo.

"Yes," said Mother Kangaroo.

"Yes," said five little kangaroos.

But the last little kangaroo cried, "Look!" And he waved his new, long tail.

His brothers and sisters began to laugh, but when they saw how much better he could run and jump, they soon wanted long tails too.

And from that time to this very day, there has never been a kangaroo without one!

The Greedy Farmer

It was nearly dark by the time poor Farmer Idris finished milking his cows. He yawned and he stretched and he made his way slowly from his ramshackle barn to his tumbledown house. Another day of hard work done – and very little to show for it.

But at the side of the cool, blue lake that bordered Farmer Idris' land, another farmer's work had just begun. The sun had barely dropped behind the hills when the Fairy of the Lake walked slowly out of the water.

She was beautiful and tall, and dressed in a dripping, lake-blue gown. She sang a song – the sound bubbling out of her, cool and clear as a mountain spring. And in response to that sound, a herd of pure milk-white cows came up out of the water after her and grazed on the grass at the side of the lake.

When dawn arrived, and the sun peeped its head over the hills, she returned to the water, her cows following behind. All but one, that is, who had wandered off towards Farmer Idris' house. All that day she grazed with his cows and later that evening followed them back to his barn.

Farmer Idris was surprised to see a milk-white cow among his herd. But as she had no markings and appeared to belong to no one, he kept her and milked her with the rest.

And from that moment on, the surprises never stopped! She gave more milk in one day than his whole herd could give in a week. And the taste of it – Oh! It was richer and purer than any milk he had ever drunk. There was soft, sweet butter, as well, and smooth, golden cheese, and thick, heavy cream. And people would come from miles around to smell it, to taste it, and to buy it.

After many months, the milk-white cow gave birth to calves, and when they had grown, their milk was just as good as hers.

And so the years passed, the herd grew, and poor Farmer Idris became rich Farmer Idris. And then, sadly, greedy Farmer Idris.

"The milk-white cow is growing old," he complained to his wife, one day. "Soon she will be no good for milking. I say we fatten her up and see how much money we can get from the butcher."

"But she has been such a good cow," his wife answered. "Why not let her wander the fields and graze her days away?"

"A waste of good grass!" Farmer Idris huffed. "No, we shall fatten her up. She'll fetch good money – you'll see."

So that's what Farmer Idris did. He fattened her up till she was bigger than any cow ever seen in those parts. Then he carted her off to the butcher's – the townspeople oohing and aahing at the size and sight of her.

The butcher held her milk-white head steady. He raised his axe above her. But, just as he was about to let it fall, he heard a song echo through the valley where the little town lay. The crowd looked to the hills round about them, and there was the Fairy of the Lake standing on the highest crag, beautiful and tall in her lake-blue gown.

"Follow me, milk-white cow," she sang. "Come away, milk-white cow. Come with me to your home in the deep-blue lake."

Off ran the milk-white cow, galloping after the Fairy – up the hill and across the fields and towards the lake. And not only the cow, but her children and grandchildren as well – every milk-white cow in Farmer Idris' herd!

Farmer Idris ran after the cows, ran as fast as he could. And he caught up with them, just as they were walking into the lake – milk-white lilies blooming at the spot where each cow disappeared beneath the water.

He called for them. He begged them to return. He promised that the milk-white cow could graze happily on his fields for ever. But there was no answer. And soon, without his herd of fairy cows, the greedy farmer became poor Farmer Idris all over again.

The Generous Bird

Once upon a time there was a bird. Not a bright and beautiful kind of bird that soared across the sky. Nor a sleek and graceful kind of bird that sailed across the water. But a plain and ordinary kind of bird that stretched out its scrawny neck and pecked at the ground as it scratched along.

And as for its song – well, this bird had no song at all. No chirp. No screech. No hoot. Nothing, not a peep!

"Tell me," said the bird to the sun, one day. "What am I good for? I am not beautiful. I am not graceful. I can't even sing."

"Ah," the sun beamed back. "There is much that you are good for. You have a gift, a special gift, that belongs to no other bird. And if you look, I am sure that you will find it."

And so, the very next day, the bird set off across the wide world – knees jerking, head bobbing, droopy tail dragging behind – to find what he was good for.

At the end of the first day, he came to a village. Most of the people had gone in for the night, but there was someone still out in the street – a little, brown-haired girl who sobbed and sniffed and called out in a mournful voice, "Here Collie! Come back, Collie! Where are you, Collie?"

"What's the matter?" the bird asked the little girl.

"It's my dog," she sobbed and sniffed again. "He's run away, and I can't find him."

"Oh dear," said the bird, sadly. "If I were like other birds, I could soar up into the sky and look for him. But I'm not very good at flying, you see."

The little girl sobbed and sniffed once more. And then cried so hard that the bird thought his heart would break.

"I'll tell you what," he said. "Why don't I walk with you, and keep you company while you look for him?"

So they walked together through the night. And the little girl called out, "Collie, Collie! Come back Collie!" in her sad and mournful voice.

But Collie did not come, so they lay down, at last, behind an old fence, and the little girl grabbed the bird tight and held him for comfort the whole night long.

When the sun stuck his head over the rooftops and announced the return of morning, the little girl rubbed her eyes and then opened them. And there, standing before her, was Collie! She leaped up and hugged her dog, and then turned to thank the bird.

"I didn't do anything," he said.

"Yes you did," the little girl smiled. "You stayed with me, and you helped me feel better."

The bird left the little girl and her dog and walked for another day, knees jerking, head bobbing, droopy tail dragging behind. And he came, at last, to a town.

Everyone was asleep. Everyone, that is, but an old woman who sat alone on the ground.

"What are you staring at?" she growled at the bird.

"Nothing," he said. "You look so unhappy, that's all. If I was like other birds, I could sing you a pretty song and cheer you up."

"I don't need anybody cheering me up!" she snarled. "I don't need anybody at all!" And then she started to cry. "Who am I fooling?" she wept. "I'm all alone because I've been awful to people all my life. To my husband.

82

To my children. To my friends." And before she could finish, the sky opened up and answered her tears with tears of its own.

"You're getting all wet," said the bird. "You'll catch cold!" So he hopped up onto a nearby wall and draped his droopy tail over her head and shoulders. And that's how he spent the night, with the rain dripping down his droopy tail and the sad old woman huddled underneath.

The rain had stopped by the time the sun blinked the new day awake.

"Thank you," said the woman to the bird. And she even managed a little smile. "It's nice to know I have at least one friend in this world."

The bird set off once again, knees jerking, head bobbing, soggy tail dragging and drooping behind.

It was dark by the time he arrived at the city. But there was still plenty of noise in the city streets. So he crept into an alley to find a quiet place to sleep. But just as he was nestling down, a little boy came tearing round the corner. He was puffing and panting, and a shaft of moonlight showed his face bruised, purple and black and blue.

"What's the matter?" said the bird.

"They're after me," panted the boy. "Bullies. They've already beaten me up once and they want to do it again!"

"Oh dear," sighed the bird. "If I was like other birds, I could pick you up in my strong claws and carry you safely away. But I'm not like other birds, am I? So here's what we'll do…"

The bird hurried the boy into the darkest corner. Then he spread his wings and tail as wide as he could and wrapped them around the boy, so the bullies saw nothing but a dark lump when they rushed into the alley.

"There he is!" they shouted, and they showered the bird with bricks and rocks and stones. But when they took a closer look, one of them said, "Hey, it's not him. It's nothing but an ugly, dead bird."

The bird wasn't dead, but when the sun finally yawned his morning "hello", he was very bruised and sore. The little boy huddled beneath him, however, was safe and warm.

The boy went to say "thank you", but when he saw the bird, all he could do was point and say, "Look! You're different!"

And so he was. His back and tail were streaked purple and black and blue, and covered with delicate raindrop patterns. And when he opened his mouth to speak, out came a haunting "Col-Col-Collie" song!

"Don't you see?" beamed the sun. "Your gift was the kindness that springs from a loving heart. And now the marks of your love will be with you always – for all the world to see."

And that is how the peacock came to be the most beautiful of all the birds!

Tiger Eats a Monkey

Tiger sat silently in the shade of the tamarind tree. He was waiting. Waiting for some careless creature to wander within reach of his terrible claws.

Rabbit stood still at the top of the tamarind tree. He was watching. Watching for Tiger, of course. But he hadn't a clue that his enemy was hiding below.

Suddenly, a jumble of monkeys came tumbling across the jungle floor, breaking the silence with their hooting and scratching and screeching.

They tumbled past the tamarind tree, one by one, but the last monkey, the littlest of them all, tumbled too close to Tiger.

"Got you!" Tiger growled, as he grabbed the monkey by the tail and went to gobble him up.

"Wait just a minute!" called Rabbit from the treetop. "What do you think you're doing?"

"Eating a monkey," said Tiger, matter-of-factly. "What business is it of yours?"

"None at all," shrugged Rabbit. "As long as you don't mind looking stupid."

"Stupid?" said Tiger, puzzled. "How?"

"It's obvious, isn't it?" sighed Rabbit. "You're eating that monkey all wrong!"

Tiger looked at the monkey. The monkey looked at Tiger. They were both puzzled.

"Listen," Rabbit continued. "It's very simple. Monkeys are not meant to be shoved in the mouth and swallowed in one bite. No! Monkeys are meant to be enjoyed, bit by monkey bit. That's why you always toss a monkey in the air and catch him with your teeth – like a nut or a piece of fruit. Everybody knows that."

85

"Everybody?"
said the Tiger,
looking again at the
monkey.

"Everybody," the monkey
stammered, nodding his head and
hoping that Rabbit knew what he was doing.

"Well, I don't want to look stupid," Tiger said, at last.
"So, here goes!" And he tossed the little monkey high into the air.

"Now open your mouth and shut your eyes," called Rabbit. "This is going
to taste GRRREAT!" Quickly, he grabbed the monkey and pulled him to
safety, and dropped some bitter tamarind fruit in his place!

Tiger caught the fruit in his open mouth – it was a perfect catch! But
instead of sweet monkey meat, his mouth was filled with the strongest,
nastiest stuff he had ever tasted.

Tiger spat and hissed and howled, but the taste
would not go away.

So he raced off to the river to wash the
awful taste out of his mouth. And when
he had gone, Rabbit and the monkey
climbed down from the tree.

The monkey's family screeched
and hooted and cheered, and then
tumbled away into the jungle. And
Rabbit just smiled, happy that
Tiger still hadn't learned how
to eat a monkey!

Lazy Tom

Tom, the farmer's son, was lazy. Everybody knew it, and even he didn't mind admitting it. He knew he should have been tending to the cows, or helping out in the fields. But it was much nicer just strolling along the hedge-lined paths, chewing on a piece of straw, wasting the day away.

And then Tom heard something – a click-clacking kind of noise coming from the other side of the hedge. He thought it was a squirrel at first. Or a bird, maybe. But when it went on and on, at a strong and steady beat, he grew curious. So he crept quietly round the edge of the hedge and peeked.

It was not a squirrel. Nor any kind of bird. No, it was a tiny little man, hammering together a wee pair of shoes.

"A leprechaun!" thought Tom. "Here's my chance to find a fortune!"

Tom moved quietly towards the little fellow, not taking his eyes off him for a second. For Tom knew that to look away from a leprechaun was to give him the chance to escape. Closer and closer Tom crept. And, what with Tom fixing his eyes on the tiny man and the click-clacking of that hammer, the leprechaun did not move an inch until Tom grabbed him with both hands and hoisted him in the air.

"Gotcha!" Tom cried. And, struggle as he might, the leprechaun could not wriggle free.

"What is it you want, then?" the leprechaun sighed. "And be quick about it. There's work to be done. Not that you'd know anything about that," he added. "For if I'm not mistaken, you're Lazy Tom, the farmer's son."

"So I am!" Tom grinned. "But soon I shall be Rich Tom – and I won't have to lift a finger to do it – for I want nothing more or nothing less than for you to take me to your famous pot of gold!"

The leprechaun sighed again. "Then I shall show you where it is," he said. "Take my hand and follow me."

Tom set the leprechaun down, grabbed his hand and followed him through pasture and wood and stream. Finally, they came to a field covered with bright blue flowers. The leprechaun led Tom to a plant somewhere near the middle, and then he stopped.

"Dig under here," the leprechaun said. "And you will find my pot of gold."

"Dig?" cried Tom. "You said nothing about digging!"

"Well," answered the leprechaun. "I only promised to show you where it was. And I have done so. Now you must keep your promise and let me go!"

"All right," replied Tom. "But you must promise me one more thing." And he took a red handkerchief out of his pocket and tied it round the top of the plant. "I am going home to fetch a spade. You must promise to leave this handkerchief here until I return."

The leprechaun looked at the handkerchief. The leprechaun looked at Tom.

88

Then he grinned a little grin and nodded his little head.

"That I promise, as well," he agreed. And then he disappeared.

Tom hurried back to his house, and after much asking (for he hadn't a clue where the tools were), he found a shovel. Then he hurried even more quickly back to the field. Through pasture and wood and stream he raced. He had never worked so hard in his life! But when, at last, he reached the field of bright blue flowers, he stopped his running, dropped his shovel, and stared.

The leprechaun had kept his promise. Tom's handkerchief was still tied to one of the blue flowers. But there were also handkerchiefs tied to all the other plants in that vast field – hundreds and hundreds of them, so that Tom had no idea which one belonged to him!

He could have dug them all up. But he was Lazy Tom, after all. So he shrugged his shoulders, and picked up his shovel. And, to the chirping of the birds and the chattering of the squirrels and the click-clacking of one sly little leprechaun shoemaker, he stumbled off towards home.

The Contented Priest

Once upon a time, there lived a fat and contented priest who served a skinny little king.

"I am much richer than you!" the king moaned to the priest, one day. "Yet, look at me. I am nothing more than a sad bag of skin and bones. How is it that you came to be so happy and hearty and round?"

"It's very simple," the priest chuckled. "You worry over many things: collecting your taxes and waging your wars. It's the worry that makes you thin. As for me, I simply trust that God will take care of everything I need."

"It's that simple, is it?" the king sneered. "Then I shall give you something to worry about, and we'll see how happy and hearty you remain. In three days' time, you must return to my palace and give me the answers to the following three questions: What am I worth? Where is the middle of the earth? And what am I thinking? Answer correctly, and you shall have your weight in gold. Answer wrongly, and my dark dungeon will be your new home!"

The king smiled as a worried shadow fell across the fat priest's face.

"Now go!" the king commanded. "And we shall see how happy you are when you return."

All the way home, the priest worried over the king's three questions: How much is the king worth? Where is the middle of the earth? What is the king thinking? "How can I possibly answer these questions?" the priest wondered.

His head hurt. His stomach churned. And he was wet with sweat. But right then and there, he decided to worry no longer.

"I will do what I always do," he said to himself. "I will pray, and trust God to take care of me."

The priest prayed for one whole day. But no answers came.

He prayed for another day. And still no answers.

But on the third day, as he sat at his window with his head bowed, an answer came in a very strange way… There was a tapping on the glass. It was the priest's gardener.

"Excuse me, Father," the gardener said. "But I couldn't help noticing. For the last two days you have done nothing but kneel at this window. Is something wrong?"

The priest invited the gardener inside and described his most unusual problem.

The old gardener shook his head. "Those are hard questions to be sure. But I think I can help you – if you will do one thing."

"Anything!" the priest agreed.

"Lend me your priest's black robe." The priest scratched his bald head. "But my robe is far too big for you," he said. "Why, you're even smaller and skinnier than the king himself!"

91

"Exactly!" the gardener grinned.

Later that day the gardener knocked on the door of the palace. He was wrapped from top to bottom in the priest's bulky, black robe. And he wore a thick, black hood over his head.

The king was delighted when he saw him. "Look at him!" the king said gleefully to one of his guards. "Just three days of worry has made him even skinnier than me!"

But when he spoke to the man in the robe, his skinny face was grim.

"And now for the three questions," he said sternly. "Number One: How much am I worth?"

The gardener paused for a moment. And then, trying to sound as much like the priest as possible, he answered, "Twenty-nine pieces of silver – and not one penny more."

"Twenty-nine pieces of silver?" the king scoffed. "I am worth far more than that! However did you come up with such a ridiculously small amount?"

"Well, Your Majesty," the gardener replied. "Everyone knows that the Lord Jesus was sold for thirty pieces of silver. Surely you do not claim to be worth more than him?"

Now it was the king's turn to pause. "No... no... of course not," he muttered. "Well answered."

Then he looked straight at the man in the robe. "But what about the next question?" he continued. "Where is the middle of the earth?"

The gardener tapped his foot on the palace floor. "Right under here," he said confidently "And I dare you to prove me wrong!"

The king was stuck. He could not prove where the middle of the earth was any more than the gardener could. So he moved on to the final question.

"Here is one you will never get!" the king chuckled. "Tell me – what am I thinking?"

"Oh, that's easy!" the gardener chuckled back. "You think that I am the priest!"

"Of course I do," the king replied.

"Ah, but I am not!" said the gardener, throwing off the big, black robe. "But you thought I was. And so I knew exactly what you were thinking!"

The king was surprised for a second.

And then angry for another.

But when he realized how clever this little gardener had been, he smiled, and then, for the first time in a long time, he laughed. And finally he called for his treasurer.

"This man deserves his weight in gold!" the king announced. "And the priest deserves the same, for he has taught me a lesson about worry."

So the priest was saved from the dungeon.

The gardener became a wealthy man.

The king tried to worry a little less often.

And they all lived happily ever after.

Olle and the Troll

Olle had never seen a troll. He was only five years old.

"Trolls are ugly!" said his mother. "They have turnip noses and berry-bush eyebrows."

"Trolls are scary!" said his father. "Their mouths run right from ear to ear and their left hand is always a wolf's paw."

"Trolls are dangerous!" said his parents together. "The Troll of the Big Mountain stuffed our best goats in his big sack and carried them away. And if you are not careful, he will do the same to you!"

Olle had never seen a troll. But if he ever did see one, he knew exactly what he would do. He had a little wooden shield. And two boards hammered together to make a sword.

"I'll chop him to bits!" Olle boasted to his parents. "I'll take care of that Troll if he comes round here again."

"You'll do no such thing!" his father warned him. "If that Troll comes to the door, you'll keep it locked tight and call for me. And that Troll will leave you alone."

Olle had never seen a troll. But the Troll of the Big Mountain had seen him. And he decided, one day, to stuff Olle in his sack and carry him away. So he waited for Olle's parents to start their day's work, then he tramped down the Big Mountain to Olle's house.

Along the way, he disguised himself.

94

He pulled a hood over his ugly head and wrapped a bandage around his wolf-paw hand. He stooped and walked with a limp and looked for all the world like a withered old man.

The Troll banged on Olle's door, and Olle looked nervously out of the window. Olle had never seen a troll. And this visitor looked nothing like the horrible creature his parents had described.

"Who is it?" he called.

"Just an old man," lied the Troll, in a feeble little voice. "I've lost a coin on your step. My eyesight isn't what it used to be. Could you come and help me find it?"

"Oh no," said Olle. "My parents told me to stay inside, with the door locked. There is an evil, ugly troll about who likes to carry off little boys."

"Do I look like an evil, ugly troll?" the Troll asked.

"Well… no," Olle admitted. "But if you were, I'd chop you in pieces with my sword. See!" And Olle held his little weapon to the window.

"It's hard to see from out here," the Troll said. "Perhaps if you were to let me come inside…"

Olle didn't know what to do. But the old man looked harmless enough. So he opened the door.

The Troll examined the sword carefully, chuckling to himself and waiting for the right moment to grab the boy.

"The Troll stole our goats," Olle explained. "I didn't have my sword then, but if I had…"

"Goats?" interrupted the Troll. "Did you say goats? Why, just this morning, I saw a whole herd of goats, up on the Big Mountain."

"But that's where the Troll lives!" Olle exclaimed.

"I could take you there," said the Troll, slyly. "We could bring your goats back!"

"Yes, please!" Olle said. "My parents will be so surprised!"

"Indeed they will," the Troll grinned. And off they went – but not before Olle had stuck his sword in his belt and shoved a crusty chunk of bread into his pocket.

95

Olle had never seen a troll (even though there was now one walking beside him!). So, of course, he didn't know anything about troll secrets. He'd never have guessed that if a troll accepts a gift from someone, he can never do that someone any harm.

It was a long walk to the Big Mountain. And halfway there Olle got hungry. So he sat down on the grass, plucked the chunk of bread out of his pocket and tore off a piece. And, being a polite little boy, he offered a piece to the Troll.

"No. No, thank you," said the Troll, firmly (for he knew the troll secrets better than anyone). And, besides, the time had come to stuff Olle into his sack.

This, of course, had to be done in just the right way. There was no point, the Troll thought, in making off with a little boy if one could not see him struggle and scream and squirm!

And so the Troll grinned a wicked grin and said, "Tell me, Olle, what would you do if I were not an old man at all, but that ugly, evil Troll?"

Olle looked at the Troll and smiled. "That's silly," he said. "You're the nicest man I've ever met!"

Well, the Troll was so pleased with his evil joke, that he threw back his head, opened his ugly, wide mouth and roared with laughter.

And he would have laughed and laughed and laughed, if Olle had not seen this as the perfect opportunity to share what was left of his bread.

He tossed a piece – a little round ball of a piece – right into the Troll's open mouth. And, though the Troll gagged and choked and coughed, in the end there was nothing he could do but swallow the bread. And that meant, of course, that he could no longer do Olle any harm!

In fact, he did just the opposite. He led Olle to the lost goats, and watched sadly as the little boy shepherded them down the hill and out of sight.

There was a great celebration when Olle and the goats returned home. His parents were surprised. Their friends were amazed. But Olle was just a little disappointed.

"I've been all the way to the Big Mountain and back," he complained. "And I still haven't seen a troll!"

97

The Steel Man

One by one, the steel-working men huffed and puffed and struggled to lift the long steel beams. It was a contest – a contest that took place once a year in the smoky shadow of the steel mill – to prove who was the strongest man in the steel-making valley.

But as the light of the setting sun mingled with the blast-furnace soot and fire, not a man among them had yet been able to lift the heaviest beam of all.

Suddenly they heard something – Boom! Boom! Boom! Then they felt the earth shake. And finally, they saw him, tramping through the twilight, hammering the ground with his steel-tipped shoes – a giant of a man, nine feet tall at least, with hands like shovels and a head full of burnt brown hair!

He lumbered through the crowd, right up to the heaviest steel beam. Then he wrapped one hairy fist around it – and swung it up over his head!

The crowd gasped. They had never seen anyone so strong. But the big man just tilted back his head and laughed – a rumbling, tumbling sound, like steel makes as it bubbles and boils in the furnace.

"Let me introduce myself," he roared. "My father was the sun, hotter than any furnace. My mother was Mother Earth herself. And I was born in the belly of an ore-bearing mountain. For I am a man who is made of steel! And my name is Joe Magarac."

Now it was the crowd's turn to laugh. For in their language, the word "magarac" meant "donkey"!

"Laugh all you want," the big man chuckled. "Because all I want to do is eat like a donkey and work like a donkey!"

The steel-working men laughed again, and clapped and cheered. Then they gathered round Joe and introduced themselves.

But high in the steel mill, in the fancy room where the bosses worked, there was another man – the Big Boss, the man who owned the steel mill. His face was pressed to the window and, through the grime and the smoke, he could see what was going on in the yard below.

"He's a strong man." The Big Boss smiled. "So I will hire him to work for me. Then maybe I won't need to hire so many other men."

Joe started every day in the same way. He gobbled up a bucket of coal, and washed it down with a bowl of steaming, hot steel soup. Then he tramped over to the mill, picking his teeth with a hard, cold chisel.

He grabbed a pile of old railroad tracks with one arm, and ten tons of iron ore with the other. Then he carried them over to Furnace Number Nine and dumped them in. And finally he shovelled coal underneath and set the whole thing burning with a finger-snap spark.

The stuff inside the furnace started to melt. It turned red and orange and yellow and white hot. But that heat didn't bother Joe. No, he stuck his arm in there and stirred it around. "Kind of tickles," he laughed.

And then, as that stuff cooled down, thick and gooey, Joe grabbed a handful in his fist and squeezed it tight. And out between his fingers oozed four perfect steel beams!

Day by day, week by week, month by month, those beams piled up. Until the warehouses were full. And the steel yard. And, at last, the mill itself.

And that's when the Big Boss came down from his fancy room.

"Boys!" he hollered. "I got some bad news for you. Joe Magarac, here, has made so much steel, we're not gonna need any more for a while. So I want you to go home. I'll call you if I want you to work again."

The steel-working men walked slowly home. No work meant no money. And that meant no food on the table or shoes on their children's feet.

They turned and looked back at the mill. No furnace firelight dancing against the window-panes. No clouds billowing black out of the smoke-stacks. Nothing but stillness and sadness and rust.

And inside the mill there was only Joe, sitting in Furnace Number Nine, a little steel tear running down his big steel cheek.

"This is my fault," he whispered to the dirty walls. "I ate like a donkey and worked like a donkey, and now my friends have no jobs. I must do something to help them."

The clocks in the houses of the steel-working men ticked away hours and days and weeks and months. Their families were hungry. Their hopes were fading. And then, one night, just as the clock struck nine, they saw it, down in the valley – a furnace burning in the mill!

They rushed out of their houses and down the crooked hillside streets. They burst into the mill itself. And that's when they heard it – the very same sound they'd heard on the night that Joe came tramping through the

twilight – the rumbling, tumbling sound that steel makes as it bubbles and boils in the furnace.

They followed that sound, and it led them to Furnace Number Nine. And there, in the furnace, was the head of Joe Magarac, floating on a white-hot pool of steel.

"Joe! Get out of there!" they shouted.

But Joe just laughed. "Don't worry about me," he said. "I was the reason you lost your jobs. And now I'm gonna fix that. When I am all melted down, I want you to pour me out into steel beams, "cause my steel is the strongest steel there is. Then I want you to tear down this old mill and use my beams to make a new one. A bigger one. One that will make jobs for you and your children for years to come!"

The big man said, "Goodbye!" and then the head of Joc Magarac disappeared into the boiling steel and he was never seen again.

The men did what Joe told them, and the next year there was another strong man contest in the new steel yard. And the prize? It was the privilege of tending the fires in Furnace Number Nine – the furnace where Joe Magarac had sacrificed himself for everyone in the steel-making valley.

The Crafty Farmer

Farmer Yasohachi pasted the bright sign on the side of the village hall:

SUNDAY MORNING – COME AND SEE!

FARMER YASOHACHI CLIMBS TO HEAVEN!

People passed by and pointed. Some smiled. Many more laughed. But one person was not happy at all, for he was Yasohachi's master.

"Farmer Yasohachi!" shouted the master. "What are you thinking of? All the other farmers have ploughed their fields. They are ready for planting. But your field lies hard and lumpy while you waste your time with silly games!"

"Oh, they are not silly, not silly at all!" grinned Farmer Yasohachi. "Come on Sunday and see."

Sunday morning arrived, and a great crowd gathered in one corner of Yasohachi's field. Most of the people from the village were there, including Farmer Yasohachi's master.

Farmer Yasohachi set up a tall bamboo pole in the middle of the crowd. Then he bowed and smiled and started to climb up the pole.

He clambered a quarter of the way.

He clambered a third of the way.

He clambered half the way!

And then the pole began to teeter and totter, to bend and sway, until, at last, both Yasohachi and the pole fell to the ground with a crash!

Someone moaned. Someone else booed. But Yasohachi was not flustered, not at all. He dusted himself off, picked up the pole, and marched to another corner of the field.

This time, he planted the pole much deeper. He bowed once more and, as the crowd whispered and watched and shuffled their feet, he began to climb again.

A quarter of the way.

A third of the way.

Half the way.

Two thirds of the way!

But, once again, the pole began to sway. Yasohachi tried to keep his balance, but it was no use, and he fell to the ground with a crash!

"Still not deep enough," he muttered to the crowd. And, even though some of them were muttering by this time too, they followed him to yet another corner of his field.

Again Yasohachi planted the pole. Again Yasohachi bowed. Again Yasohachi started to climb. But this attempt was no better, so again Yasohachi fell to the ground with a crash!

"No. Please!" he called to the crowd, as they began to walk away. "One more chance, I beg you!"

The crowd sighed and grumbled, but, one by one, they slowly followed Yasohachi to the last corner of his field.

They huddled round and stamped their feet impatiently, and as soon as the pole again began to topple, they walked angrily away.

Yasohachi picked himself up and dusted off his dirty clothes. He was grinning from ear to ear!

"What are you smiling about, you silly man?" asked Yasohachi's master. "You could have been ploughing your field this morning, but instead you made a fool of yourself in front of the whole village!"

"Fool?" asked Yasohachi. "I don't think so. Take a good look at my field."

Yasohachi's master looked, shook his head in amazement, and looked again.

Where there had once been nothing but hard, unploughed clumps of dirt there was now a field, soft and flat and ready for planting – trampled smooth by the feet of the crowd that had come to stare at Farmer Yasohachi!

Tiger Tries to Cheat

"Help me!" cried Tiger. "Help me, somebody, please!"

Tiger was trapped. During the night, an earthquake had sent a huge boulder rolling across the front of his dark cave door. And now he couldn't get out.

"Help me! Help me, please!" he cried again.

And that's when Rabbit hopped by.

"Is that you, Tiger?" Rabbit asked.

"Of course it's me," whined Tiger. "Push the stone away and let me out!"

Rabbit pushed and pushed, but he could not move the heavy stone. No, not one bit. So he scurried off to find some help.

He found Elephant. And Buffalo. And Crocodile. And, along with Rabbit, they pushed and pushed and pushed, until they pushed that stone away.

Tiger leaped out of his cave. But instead of saying, "Thank you very much!" or, "I'm terribly grateful!", he grabbed Rabbit by the ears and shouted, "GOTCHA!"

"Wait just a minute!" Rabbit shouted to the others. "I helped Tiger out of his cave, and now he wants to eat me. I don't know about the rest of you, but I don't think this is fair!"

Elephant and Buffalo and Crocodile glanced at one another. Then they looked at Tiger.

"No," they said nervously, at last. "Not fair – not fair at all."

"But I've got him!" complained Tiger. "I've finally got him! After all these years!"

"Look," said Rabbit to them all. "Everyone knows that Tortoise is the wisest and the fairest creature in the jungle. Let's share our little problem with him."

Elephant and Buffalo and Crocodile nodded. They liked this plan.

So Tiger sighed and nodded, too. "All right," he agreed. "We'll talk to Tortoise."

So Tortoise was sent for. But as he arrived, Tiger bent down and whispered into Tortoise's ear. "This had better go my way," he growled. "It's been some time since I've had a nice bowl of tortoise soup!"

Tortoise looked at Tiger and cleared his throat. He did not like threats. No, not one bit.

"Tell me," he said. "What is your problem?"

Both Tiger and Rabbit began to explain at the same time, so Tortoise stopped them.

"Wait, it's confusing if you both speak at once. Why not show me?" he said. "Show me what happened."

"I was inside the cave," Tiger explained. "Then into the cave you go," ordered Tortoise.

"And the big boulder," explained Rabbit, "was in front of the cave door."

"Then let's have it back there again," Tortoise commanded.

So Rabbit and his friends pushed the boulder back – and trapped Tiger in the cave!

"And then what happened?" asked Tortoise.

"Well, I ran to get help," said Rabbit. "But once we had freed Tiger he grabbed me and tried to eat me."

"Ah," grinned Tortoise, his wise eyes sparkling. "So, if you had never set Tiger free, we wouldn't have a problem at all?"

"No!" Now Rabbit was grinning, too. "No, we wouldn't."

"Then I say we leave things as they are," announced Tortoise, "and solve this problem before it even starts."

Rabbit thanked Tortoise for his wise decision. Elephant and Buffalo and Crocodile agreed.

And Tiger? For all anyone knows, he may be sitting in that cave and sulking to this very day.

The Two Brothers

Once upon a time there lived two brothers. Silverio, the oldest, was very rich. He was also greedy and deceitful. Manoel was the younger, but even though he was honest and hard-working, he was very poor.

One day, when he could not bear to look at his hungry wife and children any longer, Manoel went to visit Silverio.

"Help me, please!" he begged. "If you were to give me the use of even a little of your land, I could grow enough to feed my family."

Silverio thought carefully. He had the chance to do something good. But instead he decided to play an evil trick on his poor brother.

"Yes, of course," Silverio smiled, slyly. "On the western edge of my property there is a piece of land I have just purchased from Old Tomaso. You may grow your crops on that."

Manoel bowed and thanked his brother. What he did not know was that the piece of land was a desert – good for nothing but growing thistles and weeds and straggly bushes.

The next day, Manoel and his wife went to look at the land.

"I can't believe your greedy brother is helping us," said Manoel's wife. "There must be something wrong with this land."

"Or perhaps my brother has changed," said Manoel, hopefully. "We shall see."

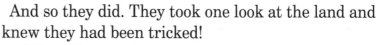

And so they did. They took one look at the land and knew they had been tricked!

"We will never feed our children from this land!" wept Manoel's wife.

But just as Manoel went to wipe away her tears, he saw something gleaming, shiny and bright, in the middle of a desert bush.

Manoel took his wife's hand, and together they walked toward the shiny thing. They thought it was an enormous gourd, but when they got closer, they saw that it was a wasps' nest – a huge wasps' nest – made entirely of gold.

Manoel's wife clapped her hands and hugged her husband tight.

"We're rich!" she shouted. "We're rich! Now we can buy a good piece of land and never again have to worry about feeding our children!"

But Manoel just stood there, quietly, shaking his head.

"My darling," he sighed. "Silverio said we could use this land. He did not say we could keep whatever we found on it. This golden wasps' nest belongs to him."

"Manoel! Manoel!" his wife complained. "Sometimes you are too honest. Your brother tried to trick us, and now we have the better of him. He need never know about this treasure."

"No," Manoel insisted. "He must. That is the right thing to do. The honest thing." So he took his wife's hand and they went to see his brother.

"A golden wasps' nest?" exclaimed Silverio, when Manoel had told him the story. "How interesting." And his greedy mind went to work at once.

"What if there are more wasps' nests?" he wondered. "And what if my brother or his wife is not so honest the next time? No, I think that I'd better keep this land for myself."

"I'll tell you what," said Silverio, at last. "I should have given you the use of a much nicer piece of land! There is a little plot to the south which is much better for growing crops."

"Thank you," said Manoel. "You are so generous!" And off he went to look at the new spot, which proved to be very good indeed.

Silverio, of course, travelled west, just as fast as his horse could carry him. But when he got there, there were no golden wasps' nests to be found. His greedy, deceitful eyes could see only ordinary grey nests.

"I've been tricked!" he grumbled. "Manoel saw that this land was a desert and made up a story so I would give him a better piece.

"Well," he grinned evilly, "we shall see who is the better trickster in this family!" And he carefully scooped one of the wasps' nests into his brown leather bag, and hurried off to Manoel's house.

"Manoel!" he called, when he arrived. "I have a wonderful surprise for you! I have brought you another of those famous wasps' nests!"

"How generous!" cried Manoel to his wife. "You see, my brother is not so bad after all!"

"Shut your windows," Silverio ordered. "We don't want anyone stealing such a valuable treasure. Now open the door, just a crack, and I shall push it in to you."

Manoel did as his brother told him, and, when everything was ready, Silverio pushed the leather bag with the wasps' nest through the doorway. Then he pulled the door shut and ran off laughing.

The angry wasps darted out of the nest and buzzed around the room. But as soon as Manoel looked on them with his honest eyes, they turned to gold and fell, clinking like coins, to the ground below! Then the nest turned to gold as well. Manoel and his family were rich at last!

The next day, Manoel went to visit his brother one more time.

Silverio was amazed. His brother was not angry. His brother was not hurt. In fact, he was smiling as he bowed and said, "Thank you for your wonderful gift."

Then Manoel hurried off, bought a huge piece of fertile land and, to his greedy brother's even greater amazement, became the wealthiest farmer in the country!

Kayoku and the Crane

Snow fell white against the black night sky.

Winter had come to the mountain where Kayoku, the woodcutter, lived with his aged mother.

"I'm cold," the old woman whispered to her son. So he scraped together what little money he had and set off the next morning to buy her a quilt in the village below.

He was halfway there when he heard a cry, and saw a crane, slender and white, held fast to the rich black earth by a hunter's cruel snare.

Kayoku felt sorry for the beautiful bird, so he took out his knife and cut the snare – string by string – until the crane was free.

Just as the bird flew away, however, the hunter who had set the trap crept up behind Kayoku.

"What do you think you're doing?" he demanded. "I worked hard to catch that bird and now you have set her free! You must pay me what she is worth."

"But I only have a little money!" Kayoku explained. "Enough to buy a quilt and no more."

"That will do nicely," the hunter grinned. And so Kayoku gave the man all the money he had.

There was no need to go to the village now, so Kayoku went straight home and told his mother what had happened. She was pleased that he had rescued the crane, and told him so, but she was still cold that night and longed for a soft, warm quilt.

Late the next day, someone knocked on Kayoku's door. It was already growing dark, so he opened the door carefully and there stood a girl – a beautiful girl – with skin white as rice and hair black as coal!

"I'm all alone!" the girl explained. "And it's getting very late. Could I possibly stay in your house for the night?"

Kayoku was at a loss for words, so he looked at his mother.

"This is a very poor house," she said.

"Especially for one so beautiful as you!" Kayoku added, shyly.

"But this is the only house around," the girl pleaded. "And it will be dark soon."

"Yes, yes," Kayoku said, at last. "If you do not mind our humble little dwelling, we will be happy to welcome you."

So the beautiful girl stayed the night. And all Kayoku could do was dream of her. Imagine his surprise, then, when she took him aside the next morning and asked if he would marry her!

"But I am just a poor woodcutter," he said. "And you… you are beautiful enough to be a princess!"

"But it is you I love," she said. "Your kind face. Your generous heart. It would make me so happy to be your wife."

So Kayoku asked his mother and soon he and the beautiful girl were married. But even though they were very happy, the winter dragged on and on, and Kayoku's mother still had no quilt.

One bitter morning, Kayoku's wife took him aside and said very solemnly, "I am going to make a quilt for your mother. I will go into my room. I will stay there for three days. And you must promise not to come in and disturb me."

Kayoku thought this was strange, but he promised anyway, And three days later, his wife came out of the room. She looked pale and thin and tired. But in her hands she held the most amazing quilt Kayoku had ever seen. It was white – white as rice – and it was made entirely of feathers!

"What a beautiful quilt!" Kayoku's mother exclaimed. "But it is far too grand for the likes of us."

"It is a quilt of a thousand feathers," Kayoku's wife explained. "And if we take it and sell it to the lord down in the village, I am sure he will give us enough money to buy plenty of ordinary quilts – and much more besides."

So Kayoku took the quilt to the village and showed it to the lord. And not only did the lord give him two thousand gold pieces for it, he asked for another one as well.

"I… I don't know about that," Kayoku stammered. "It makes my wife very thin and tired."

But the lord would not take "no" for an answer. "Bring me another quilt," he said sternly. "Or there will be trouble for you and your whole family!"

So Kayoku returned to his little house on the mountain, glad for the gold jingle-jangling in his money bag, but worried about what the lord's demands would mean for his beautiful wife.

It was just as he feared. When he told his wife that the lord wanted another quilt, he could see the weariness in her eyes.

"This one will take a week," she sighed. "And, once again, you must promise not to enter the room."

Kayoku promised and, as he watched his wife shut the door, he could only think of how much he truly loved her.

He waited one day, two days, three days.

He waited four days, five days, and six.

But in the middle of the seventh day, Kayoku could stand it no longer. He called his wife's name, but there was no answer. He banged on the door – there was no answer still. And so, unable to control his worry and his fear, Kayoku threw the door open, and gasped at what he saw!

For standing in front of him was not his wife at all, but a tall slender crane, plucked clean of every feather. And at the crane's feet lay another beautiful quilt.

"I am the crane you saved from the hunter's snare," the bird explained. "Out of gratitude for your kindness, I took the shape of a beautiful girl and vowed to be your wife forever. But now... now you have seen my true shape. And so, sadly, I must leave you."

And with that, the window flew open and a flock of cranes filled the room. They wrapped their wings around the naked crane and carried her off into the sky until they looked no bigger than snowflakes, delicate and white, against the black mountainside.

And even though Kayoku sold the second quilt and became a wealthy man, he felt poor forevermore, for he never saw his beautiful crane-wife again.

113

The Two Sisters

There once lived a woman with two daughters. The oldest was rude and bad-tempered, much like the mother herself. But the youngest was kind and gentle. And for that reason, the other two women took advantage of her and forced her to do the hardest housework.

"Take this bucket!" the mother shouted at her younger daughter, one day. "And bring us fresh water from the well!"

Unfortunately, the well was an hour's walk away. And the bucket was very heavy. But the younger daughter smiled and did as she was told.

She picked up the bucket. She walked and walked and walked. And when she came at last to the well, she filled the bucket with water and started for home.

Along the way, she met an old woman.

"I am so thirsty, my dear," the old woman begged. "And I have no bucket of my own. Could you, perhaps, give me a drink from yours?" The younger daughter felt sorry for the old woman.

"Of course!" she said. "Here, let me help you." And she lifted the heavy bucket to the old woman's lips.

What she did not know, however, was that the old woman was really a fairy in disguise!

114

"Thank you, my dear," said the old woman, as she wiped her lips on her sleeve. "Your kind words and deeds are as beautiful as flowers and precious as jewels. So from now on, whenever you speak, that is what will drop from your mouth."

The younger daughter was puzzled. This was the most peculiar thing anyone had ever said to her. But she didn't want to hurt the old woman's feelings, so she smiled politely and carried her heavy bucket home.

"Where have you been?" her mother shouted, when the girl walked through the door. "We're dying of thirst!"

But when the younger daughter tried to explain, rubies and roses and daffodils and diamonds came tumbling out of her mouth!

Her mother was amazed, and immediately called for the older daughter.

"Here!" she ordered, shoving the bucket at the older daughter. "Take this bucket to the well and fill it!"

"Take it yourself!" the older daughter snapped back. "I don't do that kind of work!"

"Well you'll do it today!" her mother hissed. "And if an old woman asks you for a drink, you'll give it to her. And then jewels will fall from your mouth, too."

So the older daughter trudged off to the well, grumbling and complaining all the way. She filled her bucket and started for home. But instead of an old woman, she met a beautiful princess. It was the fairy, of course, in a very different disguise!

"I'm so thirsty," said the princess. "I don't suppose you could give me drink?"

"Who do you think I am?" snapped the older daughter. "One of your serving girls? If you want a drink, you can go and get it yourself!"

"I see," said the princess. "Your harsh words and deeds are as cruel as serpents and ugly as toads. So from now on, whenever you speak, that is what will drop from your mouth."

"Stupid woman!" thought the older daughter. But when she returned home and tried to explain what had happened, the fairy's curse came true – toads and lizards and snakes leaped out of her open mouth!

"You've tricked us!" the mother shouted at her younger daughter. "Look what you've done to your sister!"

"But it's not my fault, mother!" pleaded the girl, a precious jewel accompanying every word.

"Get out!" her mother shouted. "Get out and never come back!"

So the younger daughter left. And, while the mother and the older daughter battled with snakes and toads for the rest of their lives, the younger girl met a handsome prince who asked her to marry him.

And so she ruled at his side – with words beautiful as flowers and deeds precious as jewels – and lived happily ever after.

The Selfish Beasts

One evening, Lion, Vulture, and Hyena were chewing on an antelope.

"I've been thinking," said Lion. "The three of us are friends. We like the same kind of food. Why don't we share a house together?"

"An excellent idea!" squawked Vulture, as he picked a bone clean.

"I couldn't agree more!" yapped Hyena. "But I do think we should set some rules first. So that we don't upset each other."

"Well there's only one thing that bothers me," Lion growled. "And that's staring. I can't stand it when someone stares at me. It's so rude!"

"Oh, I don't mind that," squawked Vulture. "But it does upset me if anyone makes fun of my head-feathers. They're so beautiful and full, my pride and joy!"

"What I can't stand," said Hyena, "is gossip! I'm not perfect. I'll admit that. My front legs are longer than my back ones. But when I find out that the other animals have been talking about me, it drives me crazy!"

So Lion, Vulture, and Hyena built a home together. And the next morning, while Lion yawned and Vulture cooked breakfast, Hyena went out for a walk.

But as soon as he stepped out of the door, Lion said to Vulture, "I don't know why Hyena is so sensitive about his legs. Surely it would be much worse if they were ALL short!"

What Lion didn't know was that Hyena had not walked very far. He heard what Lion said about him and came rushing back through the door. But he didn't say a thing. He just stared at Lion angrily and growled.

"What did I tell you?" Lion roared. "I can't abide staring!"

"And I can't stand gossip!" Hyena snapped back.

And so they began to claw and bite and wrestle and fight.

Vulture tried to stay out of it, but when
Lion kicked over his cooking pot and sent
the hot coals flying at Vulture's head, he too
became angry and joined the battle.

"Enough! Enough!" roared Lion at last. "It is
clear that we cannot live together. We must go our
separate ways and never meet again."

The other two licked their wounds and nodded in agreement. And the
three of them left the little house for good.

And so, even to this day, Lion always eats alone. When he has had
enough, he leaves. And then, and only then, does Hyena come to gnaw what
is left.

And Vulture? Vulture only comes floating down from the sky when
Hyena is gone – to pick at the bones and sing his sad, squawking song.
For when the hot coals landed on Vulture, they burnt away his beautiful
head-feathers and left him bald forever!

The Determined Frog

Splish and splash. Jump and croak. Frog hopped in and out of the muddy pond.

His mother was there. His father, too. And all twenty-seven brothers and sisters – diving and swimming and paddling about.

"There must be more to life than this muddy pond," Frog said to himself, one day.

So, splish and splash, jump and croak, he hopped away from the pond and across the farmyard.

He passed the pen where the pigs lay, and the little hut where the chickens clucked. And came, at last, to the barn.

"Now this is interesting," he thought. And Frog hopped inside.

The barn was huge! The barn was empty! So he spent the whole day hopping – from here to hay, and hay to there. And, as the sun slipped beneath the window-sills and sent the shadows lengthening, Frog took one last, long leap – and landed, KERPLUNK, in a pitcher of cream!

Splish and splash. Jump and croak.

"Oh dear," thought Frog. "This is the strangest water I ever swam in. And the slipperiest, too!"

Frog tried to climb out of the pitcher, but he kept slipping back down the sides. And, because the pitcher was so deep, he could not push his feet against the bottom and jump out either.

"I'm stuck here!" Frog realized at last. And then he croaked and croaked for help. But the barn was still empty. It was dark outside, now. And his family was far away.

Splish and splash. Jump and croak.

Frog paddled and paddled, trying hard to keep his head above the cream. But he knew that, sooner or later, his strength would give out and he would slip to the bottom of the pitcher and drown.

So Frog thought and thought. He thought of his mother, and how he would miss her happy croaking in the morning.

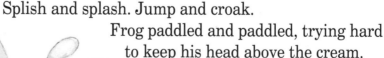

"I can't give up and I won't give up!" Frog grunted to himself. And he paddled even harder.

Then Frog thought of his father, and how they would never again catch flies together with their long, sticky tongues.

"I can't give up and I won't give up!" Frog grunted again. And he paddled harder still.

Finally, Frog thought of his brothers and sisters, and how he would miss playing hop-tag and web-tackle with them.

"I CAN'T GIVE UP AND I WON'T GIVE UP!" Frog grunted and shouted and groaned. Then he paddled as hard as he could.

And that's when Frog's feet felt something. The cream under his webbed toes was no longer wet and slippery. Instead, it was hard and lumpy. For with all his paddling, Frog had churned that cream into butter!

Frog rested his feet against the butter. He pushed hard with his strong back legs. And with a grunt and a shove, he leaped out of the pitcher and onto the barn floor.

Then the frog who would not give up hopped straight back home, and lived happily ever after, splishing and splashing, jumping and croaking, with his family in the muddy pond.

The Robber and the Monk

Once there was a monk. A little monk who lived by himself in a little clay hut. He prayed. He wove baskets from palm leaves. And when people from the city came to visit, he tried to help them with their problems.

The little monk wore a coarse brown robe, ate bread and broth, and had almost nothing to call his own. Except for a book – a very special book – which he treasured and read every day.

One day, a robber came to visit the monk. A big robber. A bad robber. With a great, bushy beard and a long, sharp sword.

"Give me your treasure!" he shouted. So the little monk gave him the book – the very special book – and watched sadly as the robber rode away.

When the robber reached the city, he went to see a shopkeeper.

"I have no use for books!" he complained. "I need gold – and lots of it! Tell me what this book is worth, and I shall sell it."

"I cannot say," said the shopkeeper, flicking through the pages. "But I know someone who can. Leave it with me for a day or two, and I will ask him."

"All right!" growled the robber, pulling out his sword. "I will return in two days. Make sure the book is here when I get back!"

Later that day, when the shop had closed, the shopkeeper climbed on his donkey and rode out into the desert. He rode for mile after dusty mile until he came at last to a little clay hut. And he went in to visit the little monk!

"I have a book," he explained. "A big man with a bushy beard brought it to me. He wants to sell it. Can you tell me how much it is worth?" Then he pulled the book out of his bag and showed it to the monk.

The little monk stared at the book. He had never imagined that he would see his treasure again. But he did not grab for it and shout, "This is mine!" or point his finger at the shopkeeper and say, "Your customer is a thief!"

No, all he said was, "This is a very valuable book, worth a year's wages, at least." Then he bid the shopkeeper farewell.

When the robber returned to the city, he was in a terrible mood.

"So tell me," he grunted. "How much is my book worth?"

"A great deal!" grinned the shopkeeper. "A year's wages, at least!"

The robber's mood changed at once.

"Excellent!" he smiled. "And... how can you be sure of that?"

"That's easy," explained the shopkeeper. "There is a little monk who lives out in the desert, in a little clay hut. He knows all about these things. I took the book and I showed it to him!"

The robber's mood changed once again. "A little monk?" he stammered. "Out in the desert?"

"That's right."

"And you told him I wanted to sell the book?"

"A big man with a bushy beard – that's what I said."

"And he said nothing more about the book? Nothing about me?"

"No, of course not. Why should he?" asked the shopkeeper.

"No reason," lied the robber. "No reason at all."

Then he grabbed the book, and dashed out of the shop – as quick as a thief!

He rode out into the desert, mile after dusty mile, until he came to the little clay hut.

"What is this all about?" he shouted, as he burst through the door. "You could have turned me in and had me arrested. But instead you said nothing!"

"That's right," the monk nodded. "For I had already forgiven you."

"Forgiven me?" the robber cried. "Forgiven me?" And then his voice grew very quiet. "No one has ever forgiven me!" he whispered. "Hated me, chased me, vowed to take revenge – yes. But forgiven? Never!"

And at that moment, something melted in the heart of the big, bad robber. He pulled the book out of his sack and gave it to the little monk.

"This is yours," he said meekly, "I can keep it no longer."

The monk smiled, and thanked the robber. He invited him to stay in the little hut – to learn more about forgiveness and peace. And it wasn't long before that robber became a monk himself who shared with others what little he had and lived happily ever after!

The Fox and the Crow

Fox crept slowly – crept up on Crow.

But as he sprang into the air – red fur flying and white teeth flashing – Crow flew away into the branches of a tall tree.

It was not Crow that Fox wanted, but the fat piece of cheese she held in her beak. So he stood thinking for a moment, and, when he had come up with another plan, Fox trotted towards the tree and called to Crow in his most pleasant voice, "Crow! Dear Crow, I'm sorry I startled you. I was just overcome, that's all."

Overcome? wondered Crow silently. And she stared at Fox, confused.

"How else can I put it?" Fox said. "It is rare that one stumbles upon such beauty as yours in this rough and ordinary world."

Crow stared, more puzzled than ever. Beauty? Me? she wondered. And she went to fly away.

"I can tell by your expression," Fox continued, "that you are not following my meaning. Stay with me, just a moment, and I will explain.

"I have seen crows before. Many crows, in fact. But none with such shiny feathers as yours. None with such shapely wings. And certainly none with such deep black eyes."

Crow could not hide her pleasure! This was all a surprise to her. But a wonderful surprise, to be sure. She wanted to say, "Go on. More please!" But there was the cheese to consider and, besides, Fox showed no signs of stopping!

"It is not only your appearance that has touched me," he went on, "but your considerable talent as well. Most birds of your kind would have launched themselves clumsily from the ground. But you soared! The graceful arc of your wings was a picture – no, a poem! – against the evening sky!"

Crow was trembling now, overwhelmed by Fox's flattery. And so she was totally unprepared for what came next.

"Dare I say it?" Fox whispered. "Is it too much to hope for? But is it possible, just possible, that flying is not your only gift? Is it possible that you can also… sing?

"If so, then I would love nothing more than to hear you. Could you…? Would you… (Dare I even suggest such a thing?) … honour me with just one note from that lovely crow throat?"

Crow could no longer think. She was so taken in by Fox's sweet words that she forgot even the simplest thing – that crows cannot sing. Not even one note.

So Crow opened her mouth, and two things happened.

The most awful "squawk" came out of her beak. And the cheese came out as well!

In fact, it dropped straight to the ground, where Fox gobbled it down in one bite.

"Thank you very kindly," he grinned. "I knew something wonderful would come out of that mouth of yours."

Then he trotted off into the forest, leaving Crow feeling foolish and flattered all at the same time.

127

City Mouse
and Country Mouse

City Mouse went to visit Country Mouse.

He shut the door of his flat. He climbed into the lift.
He walked into the garage, hopped into his car and nosed
his way out onto the city streets.

He stopped at one light after another, crawling slowly past
office blocks and theatres and restaurants.

He sped up a little when he reached the suburbs. He motored
past schools and parks and shopping malls, and row after row of
houses.

Finally, City Mouse reached the country. Fields flew by, dotted
with hungry sheep. Then barns and hedgerows and trees and hills.
He drove faster and faster, slowing down only to race around the
occasional tractor. And then he stopped. For there, at the side of the
road, sat Country Mouse's cosy country cottage.

Flowers filled the front garden, and the back garden too. And there
were apple trees and pear trees, and birds singing all around.

The two friends sat in the garden and chatted. They sipped home-made
cider and shared simple country meals – bread and cheese and pickle.

But after a few days of this, City Mouse found that he was just a little
bit bored.

"This is all very pretty," he said to his friend. "But it's nothing compared to the city! There's so much to see there! So much to do! So much excitement and adventure!"

"Well, let's go then!" squeaked Country Mouse. "Let's go at once!"

So they packed their things, watered the plants and hopped into the car.

And City Mouse took Country Mouse back with him to the city.

They drove fast at first, slowing down only to race around the occasional tractor. They flew past hills and trees and hedgerows and barns, and fields dotted with hungry sheep.

They slowed down when they reached the suburbs, driving past row after row of houses. They motored past shopping malls, parks and schools. And at last they reached the city.

They were barely crawling along now – past restaurants and theatres and office blocks – stopping at one light after another.

Country Mouse pressed his long nose against the window and just stared.

"You were right!" he said, gazing up at the tall, tall buildings. "There is so much to see! So much to do! Let's start at once!"

So they parked the car in the garage and walked out onto the city streets. They tried on fancy clothes, looked at expensive jewellery and ate their dinner at a restaurant so fine that Country Mouse could not even pronounce the names of the food on the menu! But as they walked home, talking and laughing about what they had done, they were suddenly met by a gang of very big and very hungry City Cats.

"What do we do now?" asked Country Mouse.

"We run!" squeaked City Mouse. "I told you the city was exciting!"

And that's what they did, scampering this way and that, through city streets and city alleys, until they had left the City Cats far behind.

They leaned against a city building and huffed and puffed, but before they could catch their breath, they were surprised by a pack of noisy City Dogs!

"What now?" trembled Country Mouse.

"We run again!" squeaked City Mouse. "I told you the city was full of adventure!"

Over city pavements and under city cars they raced until they ducked at last into a hole in a city wall. And while the dogs barked outside, they crept along a narrow, dark passage towards a pinprick of light at the other end.

130

"I smell cheese!" squeaked Country Mouse.

"Careful!" warned City Mouse, but before he could stop him, his friend was racing to the light at the end of the hole. There was cheese, he could smell it. There was cheese, he could taste it. There was cheese! Lying there, just waiting for him, on top of a contraption made of metal and wood. But just before he could grab it, City Mouse raced to his side and pushed Country Mouse out of the way. And the metal sprang up from the wood and chopped the cheese in half!

"City cheese board?" asked Country Mouse.

"City mousetrap," answered his friend. "I think it's time we went home." So the two friends crept carefully back to City Mouse's flat.

City Mouse slept soundly that night. But Country Mouse tossed and turned. At first, the noise of the traffic kept him awake, but when, at last, he fell asleep, his dreams were filled with cats' teeth and dog growls and the "snap" of waiting traps.

When morning came, City Mouse crawled out of bed and found his friend packing his bags.

"I'm going home," said Country Mouse. "The city may be exciting. It may be filled with adventure. But it's also very dangerous! And I think I would be happier in the country, where I belong."

City Mouse was sad to see his friend go, but he understood, he really did. For he was much happier where he belonged as well.

So the two friends locked up the flat and climbed in the lift and went down to the garage. They hopped into the car. And, crawling through the city, motoring through the suburbs and flying through the country, City Mouse took his friend back home.

Why the Cat Falls on Her Feet

Manabozho walked silently on two feet through the forest. He spied Eagle soaring, two wings wide above the tree tops. He caught Spider skittering, eight feet dancing through the fallen leaves. But he did not hear his enemy, Snake, slithering on no feet behind him more silently still.

"Manabozho thinks he is strong," Snake hissed to himself, "because he walks tall on his two feet. But when he tires, and when he lies down – level with me, on no feet at all – then we shall see who is the strongest!"

Manabozho walked all day. But when, at last, the sun wandered beneath the reach of Eagle's wings, and then beneath the tree tops too, Manabozho leaned his spear against the trunk of an oak and lay down upon the ground.

He said goodnight to Ant, six legs struggling to carry a tiny seed. He winked at waking Possum, hanging one-tail from a nearby branch. But when Manabozho closed his eyes, Snake slipped silently to his side.

Snake reared back his head. Snake opened his mouth. Snake showed his sharp and poisonous fangs. But just as Snake was ready to strike, someone struck him from behind.

It was Cat, who had been hiding in the branches of the tall oak. Cat, who had seen what Snake was about to do and leaped, four feet flying, to stop him.

Cat landed on Snake's back and dug four sets of claws into his shiny skin. He turned to bite her, but she was too quick. Again and again she leaped, claws flashing, screeching and scratching until Manabozho was awakened by her cries. He jumped to his feet, and reached for his spear. But by then, the battle was over. Snake was dead, and Cat stood trembling on her four feet beside him.

"Such bravery must be rewarded!" Manabozho declared. "With your four feet, you have saved my life, and so from this time on, wherever you fall, you will always land on your feet – and those four feet will save *you* as well!"

133

Big Jack, Little Jack and the Donkey

Big Jack and Little Jack were going to the market. They were going to sell their donkey.

They wanted him to look healthy.

They wanted him to look fit.

They wanted him to fetch the very best price.

So they tied his legs together, slipped a pole between them, hoisted the pole up onto their shoulders and set off for the market.

Along the way, they passed an old woman.

"That is the silliest thing I ever saw!" she said.

"Carrying a donkey to the market! Surely the donkey should be carrying you!"

Big Jack looked at Little Jack.

134

Little Jack looked back.

It seemed a sensible suggestion.

So they untied the donkey. Little Jack climbed onto the donkey's back. Big Jack walked behind. And they set off again for the market.

But, along the way, they passed an old man.

"That is the silliest thing I ever saw!" he said. "A strong, young lad rides on a donkey, while his poor old father has to walk behind. Surely the boy should walk!"

Big Jack looked at Little Jack.

Little Jack looked back.

It seemed a sensible suggestion. So Little Jack jumped off the donkey's back. And Big Jack jumped on. And they set off again for the market.

But, along the way, they passed a girl.

"That is the silliest thing I ever saw!" she said. "A father rides while his poor son walks. Surely the boy should ride as well!"

Big Jack looked at Little Jack.

Little Jack looked back.

It seemed a sensible suggestion. So Little Jack climbed onto the donkey –

climbed on behind
Big Jack. And they set
off again for the market.

But, along the way,
they passed a boy.

"That is the silliest
thing I ever saw!" he said.
"One poor little donkey with
two people on his back. Surely you should
give that donkey a rest!"

Big Jack looked at Little Jack.

Little Jack looked back.

It seemed a sensible
suggestion. So they both climbed
down off the donkey, and set off
again for the market. But, along the
way, they met the mayor.

"That is the silliest thing I ever saw!" he said. "You two fools walk along
while you have a perfectly good donkey to ride! Surely you should put the
beast to good use!"

Big Jack looked at Little Jack.

Little Jack looked back.

They had both heard enough!

"We will show you something even sillier!" said Big Jack. And he found
another pole.

"The silliest thing you ever saw!" said Little Jack. And he tied
the donkey's legs together.

Then they slipped the pole between the donkey's legs and
hoisted the pole up onto their shoulders.

"That is silly!" said the mayor. "The silliest thing of all!"

"No," said Big Jack, shaking his head.

"The silliest thing of all is trying to make
everybody happy!"

"That's right," said Little Jack.
"Because it simply doesn't work."

And Big Jack, Little Jack and
their donkey set off again for the
market.

The Lion's Advice

Kwasi and Kwaku were friends. But, as sometimes happens with friendships, one was a better friend than the other.

Kwasi and Kwaku would go hunting. Together they would kill an antelope or a wild pig, and then divide the meat. But somehow, Kwasi would always end up with more meat than Kwaku, which made Kwaku's wife very angry.

"But he's my best friend!" Kwaku would explain to his wife. "On another day, he will surely give the bigger share to me."

But that day never came. Whether it was meat from a hunt, fruit from a tree, or even water from the local watering hole, Kwasi would always end up with more. And no matter how hard his wife argued, Kwaku would always defend his greedy friend.

137

One cool evening, Kwasi and Kwaku went hunting.

"I will say something this time," Kwaku promised himself. "And surely my friend will give me the bigger share."

But as the two friends walked slowly through the bush, there was suddenly no time for thinking. A lion leaped out of the tall grass and decided that two friends would make a much better dinner than one little antelope. Kwasi and Kwaku ran straight for a tree – it was their only chance to escape! Kwasi reached the tree first and shimmied up the trunk to the first branch. But when Kwaku – who was not very good at climbing trees – asked for a hand up, his friend refused to help!

"I'm sorry," said Kwasi. "But there's only room for one on this branch."

"There are other branches!" cried Kwaku.

"Yes," nodded Kwasi. "But you must step on this branch to get to the others. And it could break beneath the two of us – so surely it's better that one of us survives…"

"But I thought you were my friend!" shouted Kwaku, as the lion padded closer.

"I am your friend," Kwasi assured him, "and here's a bit of friendly advice. Someone once told me that a lion will not eat dead meat. So lie down, quietly, with your face to the ground.

138

And perhaps the lion will think you're dead and find something else for his supper."

Kwaku could not believe this was happening, but the lion was nearly upon him, so he threw himself, face down, to the ground, and hoped for the best.

The lion looked up at Kwasi and growled. Then he crept quietly up to Kwaku and began to sniff. He sniffed at Kwaku's feet and at his legs and at his back and at his shoulders. And finally, he sniffed for what seemed to Kwasi a very long time at Kwaku's head. Then the lion roared and shook his mane and ran away!

When he was certain that the lion would not return, Kwasi leaped down from the tree and pulled Kwaku to his feet.

"That was a lucky break!" he grinned. But Kwaku did not return his smile.

"What's the matter?" asked Kwasi, looking carefully at his friend. "I see no bite marks. As far as I could tell, the lion only sniffed at you."

"No," said Kwaku, shaking his head. "The lion did much more than that. The lion spoke to me."

"Spoke to you?" cried Kwasi, amazed.

"Yes," answered Kwaku solemnly. "The lion told me that my wife was right – I was a fool to think you were my friend. And, in future, I should choose my companions more carefully."

Then he turned and walked sadly away, leaving his companion to wonder if the lion had really spoken, or if Kwaku had finally realized that Kwasi was not truly his friend after all.

The Dog and the Wolf

One moonlit night, Wolf went out hunting. Hours passed,
and he had nothing to show for all his hard work. He was
hungry and he was tired, so he sneaked into Farmer's yard, in the
hope of finding a stray duck or chicken. But all he found was Dog!

Dog growled and bared his teeth. But before he could raise the alarm,
Wolf crept over to him and whispered, "Brother Dog, keep quiet, I beg you.
I have not come to steal. No, I simply wanted to ask about your health. It
has been so long since we've talked."

Dog could not remember ever having spoken to Wolf before. But he did
seem genuinely interested in having a conversation. And it did get lonely
out in the yard at night. So Dog stopped his growling and began, instead,
to talk.

"I'm very well, actually," he said. "Thank you for asking." And not
wanting to be rude, he asked in return, "How are you?"

Wolf glanced around the farmyard – not a chicken in sight!

"Ah well, I've had better days," he confessed.

"I can see that," Dog admitted. "You look like you haven't eaten for ages!
(Dog had a lot to learn about tact!) As for me, well, as you can plainly see,
I get plenty to eat. Dog food, twice a day – and scraps from Farmer's table!"

"Really?" said Wolf, suddenly just a little jealous.
"I had no idea."

"There's more!" Dog went on (he was enjoying this conversation!). "When I'm tired, I don't have to find some hard spot on the ground to sleep. No, I can curl up in my own little house, here!"

"A house of your own!" nodded Wolf. "Very nice." And he thought about the night before, when he'd tried to sleep, wet and shivering, in the rain.

"And if it gets too cold," Dog continued, "Farmer will often let me sleep inside, right in front of the fireplace!"

"Oooh!" sighed Wolf. "I bet that's cosy!" Now he had forgotten all about chickens and ducks. He just wanted to hear more about Dog. And Dog was happy to oblige.

"Where do I start?" he said. "Playing 'catch' in the fields. Doggie treats at Christmas. And do you see this shiny coat of mine? Farmer's wife combs it and brushes it and pulls out every burr and twig."

Wolf was impressed. So impressed, in fact, that he couldn't help blurting out, "I wish I was a dog!"

"Well, why not?" said Dog. "We need someone to watch the other side of the yard. And you've got what it takes – sharp teeth, a keen sense of smell, plus you know all the prowlers' tricks!"

"Let's go!" cried Wolf. "Let's talk to Farmer now!"

But Dog grew suddenly quiet.

"We'd best wait till morning," he said. "Farmer doesn't like to be wakened. And, besides, there's the small matter of this chain."

Wolf looked closely, and, yes, there was indeed a chain attached, at one

141

end, to a post in the ground. And fastened, at the other end, to something round Dog's neck.

"And what's that?" asked Wolf, pointing to the collar.

"That?" Dog shrugged. "That's just Farmer's way of saying that he owns me."

"Owns you?" asked Wolf. And as he said it, he started to creep slowly away.

"What's the matter?" asked Dog. "Don't you want to live here any more?"

"No thank you," said Wolf. "A full belly, a warm fireplace and a roof over my head sound very nice indeed. But they are not worth the price of my freedom!"

Then Wolf turned and ran off into the moonlit night – hungry, yes, but free.

142

The Kind Parrot

Hunter went into the jungle to hunt. He hunted for rabbits. He hunted for squirrels. He hunted for deer and monkeys and wild pigs. But every time he raised his bow, his prey jumped or ducked or scurried out of sight.

Hunter was hungry. Hunter was tired. And then Hunter saw a parrot, bright yellow and blue, in the branches of a tree. So Hunter raised his bow. And Hunter aimed straight and true. But as he went to release the arrow, Hunter heard the parrot squawking a little song:

Hunter be good. Hunter be kind.
  Spare my life and you will find
    A reward, a promise, sure and true.
      Goodness and kindness will return to you.

Hunter dropped the arrow. Hunter lowered his bow. And as he did, the parrot flew away, bright yellow and blue, into the jungle.

And that's when Hunter heard a sound. Something was running through the jungle – running right at him through the bushes and the trees. It could have been a panther, a hyena or a wolf. He could not tell. He could not see. So, afraid, he let an arrow fly. But when he went to see what he had killed, he realized that it was not an animal at all. No, it was the brother of one of the most important men in his village!

Hunter was heartbroken. He carried the man's body back to the village. He tried to explain what had happened. He told the village elders that it was an accident. But no one believed him. And so they sentenced him to die!

On that very day, however, the village was visited by the king. Hunter's wife went to the king. She explained what had happened. She begged him to save Hunter's life.

The king listened carefully to her story. And then he gave her his decision.

"I will give your husband one chance to save himself," the king said. "A test, to see if he is telling the truth. Tonight, we will have a party in the village to celebrate my visit. We will all be dressed in costumes. If your husband can pick me out of the crowd, then his life will be spared."

The woman hardly knew what to say. Her husband had a chance – yes. But how would he ever pick out the king?

As soon as the party had begun, the guards were told to bring Hunter to the middle of the village. Just as the king had said, everyone was dressed in costume. Some looked like animals. Some looked like clowns. And Hunter's wife wept when she saw that many were dressed like kings!

She looked at her husband, but Hunter just sighed. Try as he might, he could not spot the king. He lifted his eyes to heaven, to pray for help. And just at that moment, Hunter saw something else – a flash of colour, bright yellow and blue, in the branches above his head. And then he heard a squawking voice that he recognized at once:

> *Hunter be good. Hunter be kind.*
> *You spared my life and now you will find*
> *A king wearing rags, nothing shiny or new.*
> *Goodness and kindness will return to you.*

Hunter peered into the crowd, and, sure enough, there among all the fancy costumes stood someone dressed as a beggar.

"That's him!" cried Hunter. "That's the king! The one dressed in rags!"

And as soon as he'd said it, the crowd erupted in laughter.

"Ridiculous!" sniggered one of the guards.

"He's finished!" snorted another.

But when the beggar removed his rags and took off his mask, it was indeed the king.

"Set him free!" the king commanded. "A man wise enough to see a king through a beggar's robes must surely be telling the truth!"

And so Hunter's life was spared. He joined in the party, of course – he had more to celebrate than anyone there. And as he walked home with his wife, he caught sight of the parrot, bright yellow and blue. And heard the bird squawk one last time:

> *Hunter be good. Hunter be kind.*
> *Remember this day and you will find*
> *That you spared my life, I saved yours too!*
> *Goodness and kindness have returned to you.*

The Tortoise and the Hare

Tortoise was slow. Very slow.

He walked slowly. And he talked slowly. And when he ate his dinner, he chewed each bite slowly, a hundred times or more.

Hare, however, was fast. Very fast.

He never walked anywhere. He ran.

He talked so quickly that his friends hardly understood what he said.

And as for his dinner – well, he gobbled it down before anyone else could even start.

Hare liked to laugh at Tortoise.

"Slowcoach." That's what he called him. And "Slow-mo" and "Mr Slowy Slow".

Tortoise put up with this for a long time (he was slow to get angry as well). But one day, Tortoise had had enough. So he turned to Hare and said (very slowly, of course), "Why don't you race me, then?"

Hare fell over in fits of laughter. He giggled and snorted and chuckled and guffawed, all in one quick breath.

"Of course I'll race you!" he answered. "I'll run so fast you won't even see me!"

The day of the race arrived, and Hare's friends gathered round to cheer him on.

"I'll beat him! I'll crush him! I'll run him into the ground!" chattered Hare. And he spoke

so quickly that all his friends could answer was:

"Eh?"

And "Huh?"

And "What did he say?"

But they clapped him on the back and cheered anyway.

There was no one, however, to support Tortoise, because no one wanted to be seen with a loser.

So he waited patiently at the starting line, slowly stretching one leg and then another, hoping to avoid any painful tortoise cramps.

At last, someone shouted, "Ready. Steady. Go!"

Hare leaped from the line and raced off so quickly that he soon disappeared over the first hill. But Tortoise just plodded slowly along – one foot in front of the other – determined to do his best.

Mile after mile flashed by as Hare raced past cars and motorbikes and trains.

And Tortoise plodded on, step by slow step, stopping now and then to give way to the odd, passing snail.

In no time at all, the finishing line was in Hare's sight. A crowd of animals was on the other side, waiting to cheer his victory. But instead of rushing over it, he decided to have one last laugh at Tortoise's expense.

He waved to the crowd, pointed to a shady tree and then settled down for a little nap.

"I'll show them," he chuckled. "I can sleep half the day and still beat that slowcoach!"

So Hare fell asleep, while Tortoise plodded on.

Hare dreamed of Tortoise and his four short plodding legs. He dreamed of his own legs – long and strong and fast. Then he dreamed of the race and the finishing line and the cheering crowds. And then, suddenly, he was dreaming no longer. He was awake! But the crowds were, somehow, still cheering.

Hare opened his eyes and peered at the crowd. They were shouting and raising their hands in the air. But how could that be? He was still under the tree. And that's when Hare saw Tortoise – only inches away from the finishing line! And then Hare looked at the sun. It had almost dipped below the hills, for with all his dreaming he had slept the day away!

Hare leaped to his feet. He raced. He rushed. He fairly flew. But Tortoise just kept plodding. And even though Hare strained every last muscle in his long strong legs, Tortoise managed to plod over the line just a step ahead!

"It's not fair!" chattered Hare. "I was there! By the tree! You all saw me!"

"Eh?" said the crowd.

And "Huh?"

And "What did he say?"

Then everyone rushed to Tortoise and lifted him in the air, cheering and shouting his name. While Hare was left alone, huffing and puffing and complaining away, nursing one painful hare cramp!

Why Dogs Chase Cats and Cats Chase Mice

"Hear ye, hear ye!" said the king. "I have a very important announcement to make. A dog saved my life yesterday, and so, from this moment on, all dogs are to be treated with the utmost respect.

"Food and water dishes must always be full.

"Toys and balls must be bright and bouncy.

"Playing fetch is now our national sport.

"And dog-catchers are officially unemployed!"

Then the king held up a large piece of paper.

"Here is my decree!" he announced. "Signed with my name and sealed with my stamp. I am giving it to the dogs for safe keeping."

"Woof, woof!" barked the dogs, as Dalmatian trotted forward to receive the paper. This was the happiest day of their lives. And they yipped and yapped and wagged their tails in celebration.

149

But when the day came to an end, the dogs were faced with a problem. Where should they keep that very important piece of paper? The dogs sniffed and scratched, barking out the best ideas they could think of.

"Dig a hole!" suggested Dachshund.

"And bury it!" added Beagle.

"It's not a bone!" sighed Spaniel. "It's a piece of paper. The dirt will ruin it."

"I know," woofed Dalmatian, at last. "Why don't we ask the cats to take care of it? They're clever – they'll know exactly what to do!"

"Excellent idea!" woofed the others in reply, for in those days dogs and cats were great friends.

So the king's decree was given to the cats for safe keeping. And they, too, held a meeting. They stretched and spat and cleaned their claws, miaowing out the best ideas they could think of.

"Climb a tree!" suggested Siamese.

"And hide it there!" added Tabby.

"But it's a piece of paper!" moaned a Manx. "The first gust of strong wind will blow it away!"

"I know!" purred Persian. "Why don't we give it to the mice? They're very good at hiding things."

"Excellent idea!" purred the others in reply, for in those days cats and mice were great friends too.

So the king's decree was given to the mice. And because hiding was, indeed, their speciality, there was no need for a meeting. The mice simply tucked the paper away in a safe, warm mouse hole.

And that would have been the end of the story, if one little mouse had not got a bad case of the nibbles.

He could have nibbled on a bit of carpet. He could have nibbled on a bit of wood. He could have nibbled on a nice bit of cheese. But this little mouse chose, instead, to nibble on

a nice bit of paper. And, sadly, the paper he nibbled on was the king's own decree.

He only nibbled a little at first. But once he'd started nibbling, he just had to go on and on. And the nibbling didn't stop until the paper had been nibbled clean away.

Unfortunately, it was at that very moment that a particularly nasty dog-catcher found his way into the kingdom. He picked up his net and climbed out of his wagon and set to work.

But the first dog he caught howled in protest.

"You can't do this to me! The king himself has forbidden it."

"Really?" growled the dog-catcher. "Then prove it!"

So the dogs went to the cats, and the cats went to the mice. And when the mice went to the mouse hole, all they found was one fat little mouse with the odd bit of paper clinging to his nibbling teeth.

"Yow!" cried the cats, when the mice told them the sad news.

"A-woo!" howled the dogs, when they talked to the cats.

And no one was great friends with anyone any more.

So the cats chased the mice.

And the dogs chased the cats.

And the dog-catchers chased the dogs.

And, sadly, it has been that way ever since.

Rabbit and the Briar Patch

Things always seemed to go right for Rabbit. Perhaps that's because he was so clever. Or perhaps it was because he had more than his fair share of lucky rabbit's feet!

One day, however, things didn't go so well. He was just whistling his way through the fields when Fox leaped out from behind a tree and grabbed him by the throat!

"Got you now!" Fox snarled. "And there's no escape!"

Rabbit struggled and Rabbit squirmed.

Rabbit fidgeted and Rabbit fought.

And just as he was about to give up hope, Rabbit noticed a briar patch down at the end of the field.

"I suppose you're right," Rabbit sighed. "It's all over for me now. I will surely end up in your stewpot. But at least it's better than getting chucked into that old briar patch."

"Stewpot?" asked Fox. "I don't have a stewpot! And besides, making stew would just give you time to slip away. No, I intend to barbecue you, Rabbit, right here where we stand!"

"That's fine by me," said Rabbit, tossing a worried look at the edge of the field. "Stick me on a spit. Turn me over the fire. Dip me in your sweetest sauce. But please, oh please, don't chuck me into that briar patch!"

Fox glanced at the briar patch too. He couldn't imagine what was worrying Rabbit. But he had more important plans – dinner plans!

"Barbecuing's too messy!" he decided. "I think I'll make a sandwich out of you instead."

"Oh yes!" exclaimed Rabbit. "That would be wonderful! Shove me between two thick slices of bread. Lay me down on a bed of lettuce and cover me with mayonnaise. But please, oh please, don't chuck me into that briar patch!"

Fox was getting very confused now. And very hungry.

"Even a sandwich is too much trouble!" he snapped. "I believe I'll just gobble you down, right here and now!"

"That would be so thoughtful!" cried Rabbit. "Swallow me down, skin and bone. Crunch me up into a thousand itty bitty, little pieces. But please, oh please, don't chuck me into that briar patch!"

"Then that is exactly what I'll do!" howled Fox, at last. "For nothing seems to terrify you more!"

And he picked up Rabbit by both his ears, swung him around in a huge circle and chucked him right across the field and into the briar patch.

Rabbit landed with a "thud". And then out of the briar patch came the

most horrible sounds
that Fox had ever
heard.

Rabbit screamed and
Rabbit squealed.

Rabbit yelped and
Rabbit yowled.

And then everything
went suddenly silent.

Fox crept through the
field. He crept right up to
the edge of the briar patch.
All he had to do was reach in
and grab hold of his dinner.

And that's when Rabbit stuck
his head out on the far side of the
briar patch.

"I was born in the briar patch!" he
grinned.

"I was raised in the briar patch!" he grinned some more.

"And now I'll say goodbye to the briar patch!" he grinned for the last
time. "And to you too, Fox!" Then he turned and ran away, a happy rabbit
again. Maybe because he had more than his fair share of lucky rabbit's feet!
Or perhaps because he was so clever!

154

The Crocodile Brother

Once upon a time, there were two tribes who simply could not get along with each other. It started with a stolen cow, then a few missing pigs. Hard words followed, then threats. And when the eldest son of one of the chiefs was found murdered, everyone prepared for war!

The father of the murdered boy was broken-hearted. But in spite of his anger and his grief, the last thing he wanted was for other fathers to lose their sons as well. So he persuaded the elders of both tribes to come together and try to work out some peaceful solution.

At first, the meeting looked certain to fail. It started with suspicious stares and soon turned into ugly shouting.

But just before the meeting fell apart completely, the chief stood and raised his hands in the air and cried, "Crocodile!"

Everyone fell silent, each head turning this way and that, looking for the beast. And this gave the chief a chance to speak.

"There is no crocodile among us," he said softly. "Not yet, at least. But listen to my story, brothers, please. And perhaps you will see what I mean.

"Once there lived a crocodile," the chief began, "who spotted a tasty fat chicken by the side of the river. The crocodile grinned. The crocodile opened its mouth wide. The crocodile showed its rows of sharp, white teeth. But just before the crocodile snapped its jaws shut around its prey, the chicken spoke!

" 'My brother,' begged the chicken, 'please spare my life. Find something else for your supper.'

"These words surprised the crocodile. My brother? he wondered. What does the chicken mean by that? And while he wondered, the chicken slipped away.

"The next day, the crocodile spied a sleek, juicy duck. The crocodile grinned. The crocodile opened its mouth wide. The crocodile showed its rows of sharp, white teeth. But just before the crocodile snapped its jaws shut around its prey, the duck spoke!

" 'My brother,' begged the duck, 'please spare my life. Find something else for your supper.'

"Again the crocodile was shocked. Brother? he wondered. When did I become brother to a chicken and a duck? And as he tried to puzzle it out, the duck slipped away.

"The crocodile was confused. And he was getting hungrier by the hour. So he went to see his friend, the lizard. He told him about the chicken, and he told him about the duck. And as he did so, the lizard nodded and smiled.

" 'I understand completely!' answered the lizard. 'For I am your brother too!'

"'My brother?' cried the crocodile. 'How?'

" 'I was hatched from an egg,' replied the lizard. 'And so was the chicken and so was the duck.' And then he smiled at the crocodile. 'And so, my brother, were you! When you think about it, we are more alike than we ever imagined. So why should we want to eat each other?' "

His story finished, the chief turned to the elders.

"My brothers," he said, "we are just like that crocodile."

"Nonsense!" called out one of the elders. "I was never hatched from any egg!" And the elders on both sides laughed.

"No," grinned the chief. "But you have eyes and ears and hands and feet, as we all do. And a son – as many of us have as well. We are more alike than we ever imagined. So why should we devour one another in war, when we can live together in peace like brothers?"

The Boastful Toad

Bull was big. Bull was bulky. Bull was brawny and bulgy and brown. But despite his size (or, perhaps, because of it!), Bull was no bully. He was gentle and quiet and bothered no one.

Toad, on the other hand, was tiny. Tinier than Pig, tinier than Dog, tinier than Cat. And much, much tinier than Bull.

But despite his size (or, perhaps, because of it!), he never stopped saying how wonderful he was.

"I can jump much higher than you!" he boasted to Pig, who could not jump very high at all.

"That may be true," Pig grunted, "but there's no need to point it out to me."

"I can kill more flies than you!" he boasted to Dog, who had never eaten an insect in his life.

"That may be true," woofed Dog, "but nobody likes a show-off."

"I can swim much further than you!" he boasted to Cat, who hated even getting her paws wet.

"That may be true," Cat miaowed, "but you'd better be careful, Toad. Your boasting is going to get you into trouble some day!"

And then, one bright morning, Toad decided to boast to Bull.

Bull was in his field, chewing on a thick patch of weeds, when Toad hopped right up beside him.

158

Toad looked up at Bull, all big and brown and bulky. And he thought hard about his very best boasts.

Bull could jump higher than Toad, there was no doubt about that. Toad had seen him kill hundreds of flies with his tail. And as for swimming, Toad had watched Bull paddle right across the river! So none of those boasts was going to work.

And then he remembered something – a clever trick an old toad had taught him when he was hardly more than a tadpole.

"I can make myself bigger than you!" he shouted at Bull. And Bull nearly choked on his mouthful of weeds.

"That may well be true," said Bull, "but I'm going to have to see it to believe it."

So Toad looked Bull right in the eye. Then he stood up on his tippy toes and sucked in a big breath of air. And sure enough, he blew himself up to twice his size!

"That's an amazing trick," Bull nodded. But it was plain to both of them that Toad was still nowhere near as big as Bull.

"I can get bigger still!" Toad boasted.

And he sucked in an even bigger breath of air.

"Now be careful there, little fellow," warned Bull. But Toad was determined to prove that he was right. And he blew himself up to four times his size! But he was still much smaller than Bull. So he started to suck in another big breath of air.

"I think you should stop right there," said Bull.

But Toad kept on sucking in air.

"It's not important how big you are," Bull snorted. "It really isn't!"

But Toad still kept on sucking in air.

"All right. You can make yourself bigger than me. I believe it," said Bull. "Just stop. Please!"

But it was plain to Toad that he was still not big enough. Not yet. So he shut his eyes and concentrated and sucked in one more breath of air…

All the other animals heard a "bang" somewhere off in the fields. And when they went to investigate, Bull was standing there, shaking his big brown head.

"I told him to be careful," Bull sighed. "I warned him."

"I know," miaowed Cat. "I told him that his boasting would get him into trouble one day."

And so it had. For with all his boasting and puffing himself up, poor Toad had blown himself into a million tiny pieces.

The Clever Mouse Deer

The King of All Tigers in the Jungles of Java called for his tiger friends.

"There is not enough meat in the Jungles of Java!" the King of All Tigers roared.

"Not enough elephants.

"Not enough pigs.

"Not enough monkeys and apes."

So the King of All Tigers in the Jungles of Java pulled a whisker from his tiger face.

"Take this to the King of All Beasts in Borneo and tell him that we are coming.

"To eat up his elephants.

"To eat up his pigs.

"To eat up his monkeys and apes."

"And if the King of All Beasts, all the beasts in Borneo, should try and stand in our way, then tell the King of All Beasts in Borneo that we will happily eat him up too!"

So the friends of the King of All Tigers in the Jungles of Java sailed across the sea.

And when they arrived on the shores of Borneo, what did the tigers find?

A Mouse Deer, that's all – a creature both frail and small.

"The King of All Tigers in the Jungles of Java has a message for your king. Give him this whisker. Tell him we're coming – coming to eat up his meat!"

The Mouse Deer ran off into the Jungles of Borneo, wondering what to do.

For there *was* no King of All Beasts in Borneo to give the message to!

The Mouse Deer was frail. The Mouse Deer was small. But the Mouse Deer was clever as well. So she went to her friend, the porcupine, and asked her for one sharp quill.

"You're meat, and I'm meat!" the Mouse Deer explained. "And the tigers will eat us both! But if you give me just one of your quills, I think I can make them go!"

So the Mouse Deer ran back through the Jungles of Borneo with the quill between her teeth.

When she got to the shores of Borneo, the tigers were there on the beach.

"So what's the answer?" roared the tigers of Java. "What was your king's reply?"

"The answer is NO," said the Mouse Deer, shaking as she laid the quill at their feet.

"The King of All Beasts – all the beasts in Borneo – gives you his whisker too. Take it back to your king. Tell him come, if he must. But we'll fight him, that's what we'll do!"

The tigers of Java stared at the quill. They trembled at what they saw. If this was a whisker, then imagine the face to which that whisker belonged!

The whisker was huge, the whisker was pointy, the whisker was sharp and fierce!

The King of All Beasts, all the beasts in Borneo, must be some kind of monster, they guessed.

So the tigers of Java climbed back into their boat and sailed home across the sea.

And when the King of All Tigers saw the whisker, he changed his plans at once!

And that's why, today, in the Jungles of Java, you may still hear a tiger's call.

But among the beasts, the beasts of Borneo, there are no tigers at all!

The Ant and the Grasshopper

It was a sunny spring morning.

Grasshopper lay on a bed of apple blossoms, counting the birds in the sky.

Ant hurried past, seeds piled high on his back.

"Come and sit with me for a while!" called Grasshopper. "You work too hard!"

"Can't," said Ant. "Winter is coming, and I need to feed my children."

It was a hot summer afternoon.

Grasshopper lay in the shadow of a toadstool, chewing on a piece of straw.

Ant hurried past, his back bent under a grain of wheat.

"Come and sit with me for a while!" called Grasshopper. "You need the rest."

"Can't," said Ant. "Winter is coming, and I need to feed my children."

It was a crisp autumn evening.

Grasshopper lay on a pile of crunchy leaves, staring up at the stars.

Ant hurried past, struggling with a piece of apple.

"Come and sit with me for a while!" called Grasshopper. "You'll wear yourself out!"

"Can't," said Ant. "Winter is nearly here. I need to feed my children. And perhaps," he added, "perhaps you need to store up some food as well."

"I have plenty of food at the moment," Grasshopper shrugged. "I'll worry about winter when it comes."

It was a bitter winter night.

Grasshopper huddled, hungry, between a stone and the trunk of a bare-branched tree, wishing he had something to eat.

Ant hurried past, straining against the winter wind.

"Come and sit with me for a while!" called Grasshopper. "And perhaps you could spare me something to eat."

"Can't," said Ant sadly. "I wish I could, but I can't. I worked all through the spring and the summer and the autumn, and still have barely enough to feed my children. If only you had worked a little – and thought a little more about the future – then you would have something to eat as well."

Big Jack, Little Jack and the Farmer

Big Jack and Little Jack were going to market.

Along the way, they passed the house of their friend Farmer Fred. So they stopped by to ask if there was anything he needed.

But Farmer Fred wasn't in the house. And he wasn't in the barn. And he wasn't in the farmyard either.

Big Jack and Little Jack were just about to leave, in fact, when they heard whooping and hollering from the hen house.

So they followed the sound, and that's where they found Farmer Fred, jumping up and down for joy, with something bright and shiny in his hand.

"Take a look at this, boys!" he shouted. "Then shake the hand of the luckiest man you ever met. 'Cause my chicken here has just laid me a golden egg!"

Big Jack shook Farmer Fred's hand. And Little Jack did too. Then they just stood and stared at that chicken. And stood and stared even harder at that golden egg.

"Can we fetch you anything from the market?" asked Big Jack at last.

"We're on our way there," added Little Jack.

"No thank you, boys," grinned Farmer Fred. "I reckon I'll be doing a different kind of shopping from now on. But I appreciate the offer." And then Farmer Fred got a funny look in his eye and added, "And I'd appreciate it if you'd keep quiet about this chicken of mine too!"

The next week, Big Jack and Little Jack went to market again.
      Along the way, they passed the house of their friend Farmer Fred. So they stopped by, just in case he needed something.
      But he wasn't in the house. It was filled with painters and decorators.
            And he wasn't in the barn. It was crammed full of brand-new cars.
            And he wasn't in the farmyard either. Because there wasn't any farmyard any more – just a great big swimming pool!
            So they looked in the hen house.

And there was Farmer Fred, with the very special chicken on his lap.

"I know what you boys want!" he snapped. "You're the only ones who know about my golden eggs. Well, you're not getting any, d'you hear?"

"We don't want your golden eggs," said Big Jack.

"No," added Little Jack. "We just wondered if you wanted anything from the market."

"No, I don't. Leave me alone!" shouted Farmer Fred. "I'm the luckiest man you've ever met. And I've got everything I need right here!"

So Big Jack shrugged his shoulders. And Little Jack did too. Then they left Farmer Fred with his chicken and headed down the road to market.

One week went by. Then two weeks. Then three. And, when Big Jack and Little Jack went to market, they passed Farmer Fred's house without stopping.

But on the fourth week, as they passed by, they heard a sad and sorrowful cry.

They looked in the house. It was beautiful! But Farmer Fred wasn't there.

They looked in the barn. The cars were bright and shiny! But he wasn't there either.

They looked in the swimming pool, where the farmyard had been. Still no sign of Farmer Fred.

So, finally, they looked in the hen house. And there he was, staring at a pile of feathers.

"What's the matter?" asked Big Jack.

"Where's your chicken?" added Little Jack.

And Farmer Fred just sobbed and pointed at the pile of feathers.

"Did a fox do that?" asked Big Jack.

"Or a hawk?" asked Little Jack.

"No," sighed Farmer Fred. "I did it myself. I was the luckiest man in the world. But I got tired of waiting for those golden eggs. There were things I needed to buy. So I thought that if I cut her open, I could get all the eggs at once!"

"But there were no eggs inside, were there?" asked Big Jack.

"No eggs at all?" added Little Jack.

"No," sighed Farmer Fred, "and now there won't be any more eggs, either."

"Well at least you have a nice house," said Big Jack.

"And lots of cars. And a swimming pool!" added Little Jack.

"I suppose so," sighed Farmer Fred. "But I wanted so much more!"

"Can we fetch something for you, then?" asked Big Jack.

"We're on our way to the market," added Little Jack.

"No, I'll be fine," sighed Farmer Fred.

So Big Jack and Little Jack headed for the market. But not before they'd said goodbye to "the luckiest man in the world".

Three Days of the Dragon

Once there was a river that flowed between two tribes – the Tiana and the Aroman.

When the river flowed fast and full, both tribes drank from it – and lived in peace. But when, one year, the water flowed slow and shallow, and there was not enough to drink, the peace turned quickly to war.

Warriors on both sides died. And so Tiana-Rom, chief of the Tiana tribe, came to his elders with an idea.

"The legends say there is a dragon in the far mountains. A dragon who will help any tribe that is willing to sacrifice the life of a brave young girl."

All eyes stared at him in horror, for every elder knew that the chief's own daughter, Tiana-Mori, was the bravest girl in the tribe.

"Yes," he nodded. "I have spoken to her. And my daughter is willing."

The elders looked at one another. With the dragon's help they would surely win. And so, sadly, they agreed.

Tiana-Mori left the next morning. She walked for three days, and finally she came to the dragon's cave. The dragon lay sleeping – the most beautiful creature Tiana-Mori had ever seen. His scales shimmered green and gold, and on top of his head – like a cockerel's comb – ran a ridge of bright red horns.

The dragon opened one green eye. "Is there something you want?" he muttered.

170

"There is," said the girl. "I am the bravest girl in the Tiana tribe. I am here to sacrifice myself so that you will help us defeat our enemy."

"The bravest girl?" said the dragon. "Climb onto my head, and we'll see about that."

Tiana-Mori walked slowly towards the dragon. She climbed past his sharp teeth, up his long nose, and finally onto his head.

"Now sit between the horns," said the dragon. "And hold on tight!"

And without another word, up the dragon flew – high above the mountains, so swiftly that Tiana-Mori could hardly catch her breath.

At first, Tiana-Mori thought that the dragon meant to drop her. But, as she watched the ground below, she realized that he was doing something else – something even more awful. He was taking her home! They landed just outside the village and, as everyone ran to meet them, Tiana-Mori pleaded with the dragon.

"Eat me now!" she cried. "Spare my father from the sight of the thing you must do!"

"Eat you?" said the dragon. "Wherever did you get that idea?"

"The legends," answered Tiana-Mori.

"The legends?" snorted the dragon. "I don't care about legends. There is more than one way to win the help of a dragon. And you have done so with your bravery. Now tell your people that I will help them."

Tiana-Mori scrambled down from the dragon's head and ran to her father to tell him the whole story. At once, he gathered the elders together to make their war plans.

As a reward for her bravery, Tiana-Mori was invited to the meeting too. Then she went to find the dragon and tell him everything that she had heard.

But the dragon was not interested. He was lying on his back, while the Tiana children bounced on his belly, and their mothers watched and laughed.

"Dragon!" cried Tiana-Mori. "Don't you care about our plans? You and you alone can win the hearts of our warriors and lead them to victory!"

The dragon looked straight into Tiana-Mori's eyes.

"There is more than one way to win the heart of a people," he said. "Listen to the laughter of the children. Then go and ask your warriors if they really want to turn that laughter into tears."

"I don't understand!" shouted Tiana-Mori. "Are you saying you no longer want to defeat our enemy?"

"I have promised. And I will help," the dragon grinned. "If all goes well tomorrow, the Aroman will no longer be your enemy. And perhaps then you will understand." Then, to the cheers of the children below, he flew up into the evening sky.

The next morning dawned drizzling and grey, and the dragon listened patiently to Tiana-Rom.

"Go before us," said the chief. "Terrify our enemy. Then stretch yourself over the river bed and be the bridge we cross to crush them!"

Everything went to plan, at first. The dragon stomped out in front of the Tiana warriors and the Aroman warriors shook with fear. But when the dragon reached the middle of the river, he stopped. He stood between the two tribes. And he spoke: "People of Tiana! People of Aroman! Once you lived in peace. You can live that way again! I have come to show you how."

"Peace?" cried Tiana-Rom. "When we are so close to victory? Never!"

And in his rage, Tiana-Rom let one arrow fly – an arrow that struck the Aroman chief and killed him where he stood.

"See!" he shouted to the dragon. "The legends were right. This is what you have come for – not for peace, but to help us defeat our enemy!"

And so pleased was Tiana-Rom that he did not see the arrow shot in return – the arrow that would surely have pierced his own heart, had someone not leaped in the way.

"Tiana-Mori!" cried the chief in horror. But it was too late. His only daughter lay dying in his arms.

"The legends!" roared the dragon. "The sacrifice of a brave young girl. A dragon's help. Now I will show you what the legends really mean!"

And as the arrows flew thick and fast, and more warriors fell, the dragon tore into the sky. Higher and higher he soared, till he was but a bright speck among the dark clouds. Then he dived straight towards the earth, faster than the driving rain – until he struck the river with a mighty crash!

The force of his landing knocked the warriors from their feet. When they rose and looked, the dragon was gone, but the river was flowing fast and full!

Green and gold the water shimmered. Then a voice called out from the deep. "There is not much time. Come together to the river. Wash your dead in the water and they will live."

So that is what the tribes did. Tiana-Rom went first, carrying Tiana-Mori. And the Aroman followed with their fallen chief. And there, in the river, the warriors of Tiana and the warriors of Aroman came back to life!

But that was not all. As they waded and splashed, the people of Tiana and Aroman looked into each other's faces once again. And they remembered the days when the river was full – the days when they lived in peace. And so it was that their friendship came back to life as well.

They embraced one another, and so caught up were they in their reunion that they did not notice the bridge – a ridge of bright red horns, like a cockerel's comb – that grew from one side of the river to the other.

Later, as the tribes celebrated their peace, Tiana-Mori sat on the bridge and stared into the water.

"I'll miss you," she said. "And I'm sorry that I did not trust you. But I understand now. I really do. There's more than one way to do everything. To win the help of a dragon. To win the heart of a people."

"Yes," rose a voice from the river. "And there's more than one way to win a battle too."

How the Turkey Got Its Spots

In the African bush, there lives a wild turkey, who is covered all over with bright white spots. But it was not always so. For, once upon a time, the wild turkey was as black as night. This is the story of how the turkey got her spots.

One evening, as Turkey scratched her way through the dry and dusty bush, she spotted a young lion, creeping up on her best friend, Cow. Lion looked hungry – very hungry indeed. And Cow had no idea that he was behind her. So Turkey did the cleverest and bravest thing she could think of. She raced between Lion and Cow, wings flapping, tail dragging and kicking up clouds of dry bush dust.

Lion coughed and sneezed and tried to shake the dust from his eyes. Cow heard him and hurried away. And when the dust had settled and Lion could finally see, Cow was gone! There was no trace of her, for the dust had covered even her hoofprints.

All he could find, in fact, were a few black tail-feathers.

"Turkey!" Lion growled. And he vowed to remember what she had done.

The next evening, Turkey scratched her way to the watering hole. And there was Lion again, tail twitching, creeping closer to Cow than he had been the night before!

Once again, Turkey was determined that Lion would not have her friend for his supper. So, once again, she raced between them, wings flapping, tail dragging and kicking up clouds of dust. And, once again, Lion coughed and sneezed – and failed to catch his supper.

"Turkey!" he roared. But both she and Cow were, by then, long gone.

And so, the next evening, it was not Cow that Lion stalked. No, he went hunting for Turkey. And he found her, at last, leading her little family of chicks back to their nest.

"Gotcha!" Lion roared, as he sprang into the air and bared his claws. But Turkey was not only clever; she was also quick. And before Lion could land, she scooted out of his way, screeching and flapping her wings to send her children running for cover.

Then she pecked at Lion, first at his head, then at his shoulders and at his back. He leaped and twisted and clawed the air. And when he was thoroughly confused, she raced off into the bush, leading him away from her fleeing chicks.

As she ran, Turkey passed Cow, who was grazing behind a big bushy tree.

"Come here, my friend!" called Cow. "Come quickly!" And when they were both safely behind the tree, Cow dipped the tip of her tail into her milk and sprinkled it over her friend. Soon Turkey was no longer black, but covered all over with bright white spots!

Turkey flapped out from behind the tree, just as Lion raced by. And because she now looked so different, Lion did not know who she was!

"Have you seen Turkey?" he panted. "She's a big bird – about your size – but black all over."

Turkey shook her head. But she did not say a word, for fear that she would give herself away.

So Lion roared off again, leaving Turkey and Cow chuckling to themselves.

"Quick!" said Cow, "Fetch your chicks and I will give them spots as well."

So that's what Turkey did. And ever since, the wild turkey has not only been clever and quick, but, as a sign of her bravery and kindness, she has been covered all over with bright white spots.

The Tortoise and the Fox

Tortoise and Fox were unlikely friends.
Fox was clever and quick and sleek.
Tortoise was solid and heavy and slow.
But they laughed at each other's jokes
and enjoyed each other's company, and their
differences seemed to make no difference at all.
One evening, as they sat chatting by the riverside,
Leopard leaped out of the bushes!

Leopard was handsome and graceful and dangerous. Fox saw him at once and, because he was clever and quick, darted away from Leopard's sharp claws. But poor Tortoise was not so lucky. Because he was solid and slow, all he could do was pull his head and legs into his lumpy shell and hope for the best. Leopard scooped Tortoise up, scooped him right up out of the riverside mud. He scratched at the shell with his strong sharp claws. Inside, Tortoise shuddered. And outside, hiding safely behind a tree, Fox shuddered as well.

Then Leopard gnawed at the shell, biting down hard with his shiny white teeth. Inside, Tortoise shivered with fear. And outside, his friend Fox shivered too. The shell was lumpy and the shell was hard, but both Fox and Tortoise knew that it wouldn't be long before Leopard gnawed his way inside.

And so Fox – clever, quick Fox – called out to Leopard from behind the tree.

"Leopard, O Leopard!" he barked. "You're doing that all wrong! I'm a bit of an expert at these

things, and, if you like, I can tell you how to a eat a tortoise."

Leopard stopped his scratching and his gnawing.

"Really?" he asked.

And Tortoise, still shivering inside his shell, asked himself the same question. "Really?" he wondered. "Is my friend Fox really going to tell the Leopard how to eat me?"

Fox cleared his throat. "Right, then," he began, "your problem is that the shell is too hard. What you need to do is to soften it up a bit. And what is better for softening things than water? So simply throw Tortoise into the river, wait for the shell to soften and then you will be able to eat him!"

Leopard was handsome and graceful and dangerous. But he was not very clever. So he did exactly what Fox suggested. He threw Tortoise into the river. Just as soon as Tortoise reached the bottom, he stretched out his legs and stuck out his head, and he sneaked silently away along the muddy river bed.

"How long do I wait?" asked Leopard, unaware that his dinner was long gone.

Fox looked up through the trees at the setting sun. "Until it is dark," he answered. "The darker the better!"

So Leopard waited by the river until midnight, growing hungrier and angrier as the night wore on, until he realized he never would have his dinner.

And as for Tortoise and Fox? The two friends had one more joke to laugh about together!

The Generous Rabbit

Rabbit shivered.

Rabbit sneezed.

The snow rose up to Rabbit's nose.

Rabbit rubbed her empty belly. Rabbit was hungry and tired and cold.

Then Rabbit stumbled across two turnips near the trunk of a tall pine tree.

So she hopped for joy, picked up the turnips and carried them all the way home.

Rabbit gobbled up the first turnip. But when she got to the second, she was full.

I bet my friend Donkey could use this turnip, Rabbit thought.

So she hopped all the way to Donkey's house, and, because Donkey was not at home, she left the turnip in Donkey's dish.

Donkey was looking for food as well.

Donkey shivered.

Donkey sneezed.

The snow rose up to Donkey's knees.

Donkey rubbed his empty belly. He was tired and hungry and cold.

Then Donkey spied two potatoes, near a fence in the farmer's field.

So he gave a happy "hee-haw", picked up the potatoes and carried them home.

Donkey gobbled up both potatoes, and then he noticed that a turnip had mysteriously appeared in his dish.

Now how did that get there? Donkey wondered. And being much too full to eat it, Donkey thought of his friend Sheep.

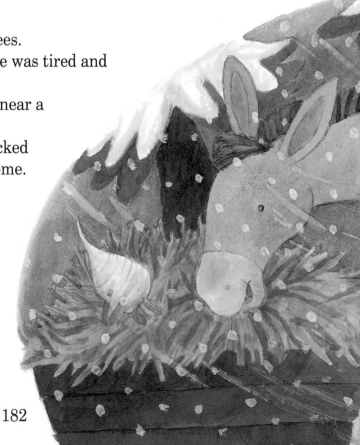

So Donkey carried the turnip to Sheep's house and, because Sheep was not at home, Donkey left the turnip on Sheep's soft bed of straw.

Sheep was looking for food as well.

Sheep shivered.

Sheep sneezed.

The snow rose up to Sheep's woolly tail.

Sheep rubbed her empty belly. She was tired and hungry and cold.

Then Sheep spotted a cabbage in the shadow of a snow-covered bush.

So she bleated a happy "Hooray!" and picked up the cabbage and carried it home.

Sheep gobbled up the cabbage. And then she noticed that a turnip had mysteriously appeared on her bed.

Now how did that get there? Sheep wondered. And, being much too full to eat it, she thought of her friend Squirrel.

So Sheep carried the turnip to Squirrel's house. And because Squirrel was not at home, she shoved the turnip into Squirrel's tree-trunk hole.

Squirrel was looking for food as well. (Just like everyone else!)

Squirrel shivered.

Squirrel sneezed.

The snow rose right up to Squirrel's ears.

Squirrel rubbed his empty belly. He was tired and hungry and cold.

And then Squirrel sniffed out a few nuts buried deep in the snowy soil.

Squirrel was so excited that he shook his bushy tail.

Then he carried the nuts
back to his house.

When he got there, however,
he couldn't get in. Someone had
shoved a turnip into his tree-
trunk hole!

Now how did that get there? Squirrel
wondered. And, as he gobbled up the nuts,
he thought of a friend, a friend who could surely
use something to eat.

So he pulled the turnip out of the hole and pushed it through
the snow, all the way... to Rabbit's house!

Rabbit was asleep, so Squirrel left the turnip by her side and
crept quietly back home.

When Rabbit awoke, she was no longer tired,
she was no longer cold. But she was hungry
again.

I wish I'd kept that extra turnip,
she thought. And when she
opened her eyes, there it was,
right beside her!

Now how did that get
here? Rabbit wondered.
Then she gobbled it up
until she was full.

The Noble Rooster

Rooster was never on time.
    His job was simple enough, really.
    Wake up early.
    Watch for the sun.
    And then cry "Cock-a-doodle-do".
    But Rooster couldn't seem to get the hang of it.
    He didn't like waking up early.
    He fell asleep as he watched for the sun.
    And that's why his "Cock-a-doodle-dos" were always late.

The other chickens never let him forget it. They clucked and cackled and flapped their disapproval as he picked his way down from the barn roof each day. And that's what he thought they were doing, one particularly bright and sunny morning.

"Sorry," he muttered.

"Late again, I know," he yawned.

"Won't happen next time," he promised.

But no one paid any attention to him. And finally, he realized that they weren't talking about him at all.

"Haven't you heard?" clucked a big brown hen. "The ogre who lives on top of the mountain has been stomping all over the farmer's crops! And he has told the farmer that the only way he will stop is if the farmer promises to give him a chicken to eat, each and every day!"

"The farmer has challenged the ogre to a contest," clucked a little yellow chick. "If the ogre can build a stairway up the mountainside in just one night, the farmer will do what he asks. But if he cannot, the ogre will leave us all in peace."

"And that's where you come in, Rooster," clucked a third chicken. "The farmer and the ogre have agreed that the contest will come to an end when the sun rises and the rooster crows. We don't want the ogre to have any more time than necessary, which means that, for once, just once, you must not be late!"

Rooster wanted to say, "I can't do it."

He wanted to beg, "Find someone else."

He wanted to shout, "No, anyone but me!"

But one look at the chickens convinced him. They were counting on him. And he was determined, this time, not to let them down.

That very night, as the sun fell behind the barn, the contest began. The chickens watched nervously as the ogre picked up the first stone step and put it in place. He was gruesome, grumpy and green. He had one horrible horn sticking out the top of his head. And he was very, very strong. But it was a long way up the mountainside, so all the hens could do was hope as, one by one, they dropped off to sleep.

Rooster, meanwhile, was hiding in a corner of the farmyard. He knew he could never wake up on time. He knew that everyone was counting on him. So he decided not to go to sleep at all. And that way, he would be sure to greet the rising sun.

He walked round and round.

He jumped up and down.

He sang little songs and played little games and splashed his face again and again with cold water. He kept himself so busy, in fact, that he did not notice when that clever ogre sneaked into the farmyard. He did not see when that clever ogre slipped a little brown hood over the head of every sleeping chicken. And he did not hear when that clever ogre chuckled quietly to himself, "Now there will be no one to crow at the rising of the sun, and I'll be sure to win!"

But there was someone left to crow – someone whose eyelids grew heavy, whose head kept dropping on his feathery chest, but who kept awake as the stone stairway grew, step by step.

And as the first ray of morning sun crept up over the edge of the hills…

And as the ogre picked up the final stone…

And as he reared back his horrible head to laugh at his clever trick and celebrate his victory with a shout, Rooster staggered to his feet and cried, "Cock-a-doodle-do!"

It was a sleepy cock-a-doodle-do.

And it was a quiet cock-a-doodle-do.

But it was a cock-a-doodle-do nonetheless.

A cock-a-doodle-do that woke the farmer and the chickens and made the ogre howl, "Nooooo!"

The farmer was delighted.

The chickens were puzzled. Why is it still dark? they wondered.

And the ogre just dropped the last stone and walked over the mountain, dejected – never to be seen again.

There was a great celebration, of course. In the farmhouse. And in the farmyard too! And even though Rooster never again managed to cry "cock-a-doodle-do" on time, no one ever complained. Because he had done his best when it really mattered.

Rabbit and the Crops

Rabbit needed to feed his family.

Rabbit wanted to grow some food.

But Rabbit didn't have any land.

So he went to Bear, who had acres and acres of it, and asked if he could use a little piece.

"No problem," said Bear, "just as long as you give me a share of everything you grow."

"What share would you like?" asked Rabbit.

Bear just grinned. "My share will be everything that grows on top of the ground. And you can keep anything that grows underneath."

Rabbit thought about this for a minute. Then he shook Bear's big brown paw. "You have a deal!" he said.

189

And Bear just grinned some more. For now he would get everything that Rabbit grew, and Rabbit would be left with nothing but the roots!

Rabbit, however, knew exactly what he was doing. He called his children together. He told them to plant the field. And a few months later, when the crops were grown, he invited Bear down to collect his share.

"Now let me get this straight," said Rabbit, as they walked together to the field. "You get what's on top of the ground? And I get what's underneath?"

"That's the deal!" Bear grinned.

So Rabbit hollered to his children, "All right then, you can dig up those potatoes!"

And the grin slipped right off Bear's brown face. For now Rabbit would get all the potatoes, and Bear would be left with nothing but the useless potato plants!

The next year, Rabbit visited Bear again.

"I'd like to plant more crops on that piece of land," he said.

Bear just grinned. He wasn't going to be fooled this time. So he reached out his big brown paw and said, "No problem. But this year, I'll take what's on the bottom, and you can have what's on top!"

Rabbit thought about this for a minute, then shook Bear's big brown paw. "It's a deal," he said. And he and his children planted the field.

A few months later, when the crops were grown, Bear came to collect his potatoes.

But all he found waiting for him was a big pile of useless straw!

"Didn't I tell you?" said Rabbit. "I decided to plant oats this year. I've cut what I need right off the top and, as we agreed, the rest is yours!"

Bear was furious. But he did not let it show. No, he stomped home, planning hard how to get even with Rabbit.

The next year, Rabbit came to visit again. But before he could even ask, Bear had his answer ready.

"No problem!" he grinned. "Of course you can plant crops in my field again. But this year, I want the tops AND the bottoms for my share!"

Rabbit thought about this for a minute. Then he held out his paw. "It's a deal!" he grinned, and went off to plant the field.

Bear was so excited about his plan that he could hardly wait for the plants to grow. So he visited Rabbit a week or two before harvest, just to see how the crops were doing.

Rabbit welcomed him and led him to the field. But when Bear saw what was growing there, all he could do was let out a big bear groan, for Rabbit had tricked him again.

"As we agreed," grinned Rabbit, "you can have the tops AND the bottoms. And I'll keep the sweetcorn – that's growing in the MIDDLE!"

The Woman and the Bird

Whack! Whack! Whack! The woman hacked at a banana tree.

High above, in the banana tree branches, a mother bird sat on her nest.

"Stop it!" she begged. "Please stop it at once!"

But all the woman could hear were the cries of some noisy bird.

So – Whack! Whack! Whack! – she kept on hacking, until finally the banana tree fell to the ground, taking the poor bird's nest along with it.

"You've wrecked my nest! You've broken my eggs!" cried the bird.

But all the woman could hear was screeching and squawking, so she slung the axe over her shoulder and headed home.

It wasn't long before the woman had a baby of her own, and the family was invited round to celebrate his birth. Pure spring water was needed for the naming ceremony, so the woman sent two of her little cousins, a boy and a girl, off into the jungle to fetch it.

When they got to the spring, there in a tree, right in front of them, sat the mother bird. She was the most beautiful bird they had ever seen, with a tail like a jewelled

fan and a crown of feathers
on top of her head.

As they watched, the bird
began to dance.

She hopped back and forth.
She bobbed her head up and
down. She shook her feathery tail.
She turned round and round and round.
And as she danced, she sang a little song:

Watch me dance,
Hear me sing,
Stay with me
At the freshwater spring.

And so the children stayed. In fact, they could do nothing
else, for with her dancing and her singing the bird had put
them into a kind of a trance!

It wasn't long before the woman wondered where the
children had gone. So she sent her brother to look for them. He
found them at the spring. But, when he saw the beautiful bird
and heard her song, he too fell into a trance and could not move.

One by one, the woman sent all her relatives to the spring. And, one by one, they were entranced by the bird and failed to return. Finally, there was no one left at the house but the woman and her baby. So she made sure that he was bundled up safely, fast asleep in his bed, and she went off into the jungle as well.

As soon as the bird saw the woman, she stopped her dancing and her singing and flew out of the tree. And all at once, the cousins and the brothers and the sisters and the nieces and the nephews and the uncles and the aunts came to their senses.

"What have you been doing?" the woman shouted.

But all any of them could remember was the bird and her dance and her song.

Frustrated, the woman got some water from the spring, then led her relatives back towards the house. But as they got near, each and every one of them heard the baby cry. They rushed to the house, and there was the bird, high on the roof, with the baby in its claws!

"Please!" cried the woman. "Do not hurt my baby! Give him back to me, please!"

The bird did not sing. The bird did not dance. No, the bird simply spoke. And because the woman was paying attention this time, she understood exactly what the bird had to say.

"I begged you not to cut down my tree," said the bird. "I begged you to

spare my nest. I begged you not to destroy my precious eggs, just as you are begging me now. But you would not listen."

"I'm listening now!" the woman cried. "What do you want me to do?"

"I want you to understand," explained the bird, "that we creatures have feelings too – birds and beasts, everything that flies or crawls or roams through the jungle. We love our homes and we love our children, just as you do. And we cannot bear to watch you destroy them."

"I understand now. I really do," called the woman. "And I promise that I will always be kind to the creatures in the jungle. But please give me back my baby. I beg you!"

The bird rose from the roof, and it looked, for a moment, as if she might fly away. But then she floated down to the woman and laid the baby at her feet.

"Thank you," the woman sobbed, as she picked up her baby and cradled him in her arms.

Then the bird spread her wings and rose into the sky. And as she flew away, she sang another song:

> *Watch me dance.*
> *Hear me sing.*
> *Be at peace*
> *With every living thing!*

The Mole's Bridegroom

The Mole Lord had a lovely mole daughter. When the time came for her to marry, he decided that she should wed nothing less than the greatest thing in all the world. So he called together the wisest moles in Japan to help him find her a husband.

The moles scratched their thin mole beards and squinted their weak mole eyes. They thought very hard. And, at last, one mole stood and spoke.

"Surely, the greatest thing in all the world," he said, "is the sun."

"That's the answer then!" exclaimed the Mole Lord. "My daughter shall marry the sun!"

"Wait just a minute," said another mole, rising to his pale mole feet. "The sun may be great. But, all around the sun, we see the sky. So, surely, that is the greatest thing in all the world."

"So be it!" declared the Mole Lord. "My daughter shall marry the sky!"

"Not so fast," said yet another mole, tapping his long mole nose. "The sky is sometimes covered by clouds. So, surely, a cloud is the greatest thing in all the world."

"Excellent!" shouted the Mole Lord. "My daughter shall marry a cloud!"

"Wait," sighed another mole, scratching his smooth mole head. "Am I not right in saying that a strong wind can blow away any cloud? So, surely, the wind must be the greatest thing in all the world!"

"Brilliant!" grinned the Mole Lord. "My daughter shall marry the wind!"

"But no matter how hard the wind blows," suggested yet another mole, "it cannot move the earth! So, surely, the earth is the greatest thing in all the world!"

"Then it's settled," declared the Mole Lord. "My daughter shall marry the earth!"

"Yes, yes, yes," muttered the oldest, greyest and wisest mole of them all. "The earth may be hard. The earth may be strong. But what can dig a hole in the earth? A mole – that's what! And so I say, surely, a mole is the greatest thing in all the world."

"Why didn't I think of that?" asked the Mole Lord. "It's so obvious!"

And that is how the daughter of the Mole Lord came to marry... a mole!

The Kind-hearted Crocodile

"So what did you boys do today?" Mama Croc asked her croc-lings.

"I ate a dingo!" shouted Colin Croc.

"I ate a dingo and his mum!" boasted his brother Clive.

And then Mama Croc turned to her youngest boy and sighed. She had tried to bring up her boys in the best Croc tradition. But, in spite of all her talk about munching and crunching and gobbling up, young Christopher had still turned out to be the kindest croc in the county!

"Well," muttered Christopher, "I found a dingo too."

"Yes?" asked Mama Croc hopefully.

"And he was crying," said Christopher.

"Because you were so big and nasty?" added Mama Croc.

"No…" hesitated Christopher. "Because he was little and scared and somebody had just eaten his brother and his mum…"

"So I pulled out my hankie and wiped his eyes and took him by the paw and helped him find his dad."

Mama Croc wept into her apron.

The Croc brothers sniggered in the corner.

And Papa Croc looked over his paper and said much the same thing he said every night.

"Go to your room! And tonight, I want you to write DINGOS ARE FOR DINNER one hundred times, before you go to bed!"

The following evening, Mama Croc tried again.

"So what did you boys do today?" she asked.

"I ate a 'roo!" shouted Colin Croc.

"I ate a 'roo and his nephew!" boasted his brother Clive.

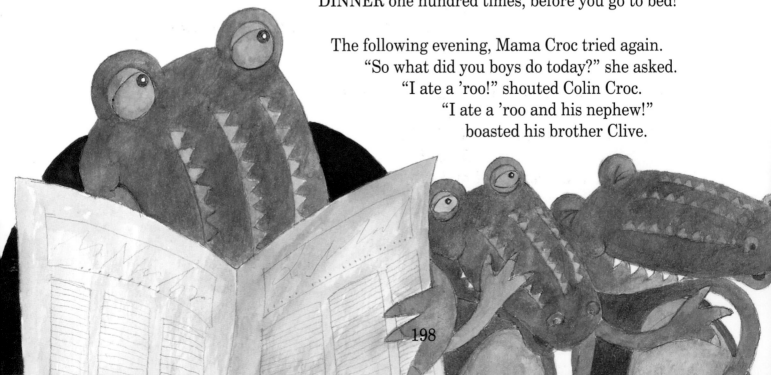

And then it was Christopher's turn.

"Well," he muttered. "I found a 'roo too."

"Yes…?" asked Mama Croc, crossing her fingers.

"And I would have eaten it and all its nieces and nephews, except…"

"Except the Croc Hunter came along and interrupted you?" hoped Mama Croc.

"Except a gigantic tidal wave swept you away?" giggled Colin Croc.

"Except you forgot your knife and fork?" suggested Clive Croc.

"Except the 'roo stubbed his big toe and you felt sorry for him," sighed Papa Croc.

"How did you guess?" moaned Christopher Croc. "And there were big tears in his eyes, as well, so I fished a plaster out of my rucksack and helped him home and had a very nice cup of tea with his gran."

Mama Croc sobbed into a towel.

The Croc brothers howled with laughter.

And Papa Croc just pointed upstairs.

"ROOS ARE FOR STEWS," he grunted. "Two hundred times. We'll see you in the morning."

It went the same way the rest of the week, as well.

"KOALAS ARE FOR KEBABING."

"GOANNAS ARE FOR GARNISHING."

"PLATYPUSES ARE FOR PICKLING."

So when Saturday arrived, Christopher Croc was determined to be anything but kind. He went out early, before anyone else was up, in search of something to frighten.

And, not two minutes later, the Croc Hunter sneaked into the house, surprised the sleeping Croc family, and bundled them all into his truck!

Christopher, meanwhile, was having no luck at all.

He growled at a 'roo.

"Nice to see you, Christopher!" she smiled.

He snapped at a platypus.

"And a good morning to you!" the platypus chirped.

He opened his mouth wide in the path of a baby bunny.

And the bunny just bounced on his tongue, laughing!

"I'll never be nasty!" he sighed. And because he was staring sadly at the ground, he walked right into the side of a house. The house of the Crocodile Hunter!

The Crocodile Hunter was every croc's enemy. This was the perfect chance to do something really nasty.

I could wreck the place! thought Christopher Croc. And teach that Crocodile Hunter a lesson!

But when he went inside, it looked as if it had already been wrecked! There were half-eaten tins of food lying about, dirty clothes everywhere, and there was dust on all the furniture.

There was no way that Christopher Croc could make that house any worse. But, as he looked around, he could think of all kinds of ways to make it better!

So he found an old broom and a crusty mop and set to work.

He washed and he scrubbed and he tidied. He even found a picture of the Croc Hunter's mum, buried under a pile of dirty dishes. So he cleaned it up and left it on the table, beside a little bunch of wild flowers. And just as he was finished, the truck pulled up outside.

There was nowhere to run, so Christopher Croc climbed into a cupboard.

Then he opened the door, just a crack, to see the hunter's reaction.

He thought the hunter might be surprised.

He hoped he would be pleased.

But he never expected what he actually saw – his entire family, tied up and gagged, at the end of the hunter's big rope!

If there was ever a time to be nasty – this was it! But before

Christopher Croc could leap out of the cupboard, the Crocodile Hunter began to sob.

He was staring at the picture of his mum – holding it between his trembling hands.

"I've missed you, Mum. I really have. I've been out in the swamps too long. And, by gum, I'm coming to see you. Not tomorrow. Not next week. But today. These Crocs'll keep. Your Billy Boy is coming home!"

And with that he scooped up the flowers, stuffed the picture inside his shirt, and ran out of the door.

When Christopher Croc heard the truck leave, he burst out of the cupboard and untied his family. At first, they were surprised to see him, and then they took a good look around the room.

"Been doing some cleaning?" asked Colin Croc.

"And some washing?" asked his brother Clive.

Christopher Croc looked at the floor. "Well…" he began.

"Well, good on ya! I say," shouted Papa Croc. "It looks like you've saved the day!"

So the Croc family headed home. And that night, the older Croc brothers had to write, three hundred times:

IT'S ALL RIGHT FOR A CROC TO BE KIND EVERY NOW AND THEN – WELL, AT LEAST WHEN YOUR FAMILY HAS BEEN CAUGHT BY A HUNTER WHO HASN'T SEEN HIS MUM FOR A WHILE.

201

Why the Tortoise Has No Hair

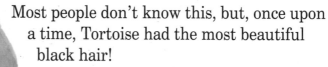

Most people don't know this, but, once upon a time, Tortoise had the most beautiful black hair!

Sometimes he would wear it piled high, in a big bouncy bouffant.

Sometimes he would comb it back, with a handful of grease – all Elvis-like.

And sometimes he would let it grow long, all the way down to his hard shell shoulders.

Tortoise loved his hair. In fact, the only thing he loved more was his breakfast.

One night, Tortoise stopped over at his mother-in-law's house. And when he stuck his head out of his shell the next morning, he smelled something that made his tortoise tummy rumble, and his thin tortoise lips dribble and drool. It was porridge – a huge hot steaming pot of porridge – bubbling away in the kitchen below.

Now, you may not like porridge. You may well be disgusted by its lumpy, gooey stickiness. But Tortoise adored porridge! Not Scottish-style porridge – savoury with butter and salt. And not American-style porridge, either – sweet with raisins and dark brown sugar. No, Tortoise adored Tortoise-style porridge – crunchy with river bugs and the odd muddy reed!

So Tortoise hurried down to breakfast. But not before he took a moment to organize his beautiful black hair. There was no time for a bouffant, and he had run out of grease, so he piled it all on top of his head, held it tight with a

couple of fancy clips, and then stuffed it under a big floppy hat.

"I'll put it up later," he promised himself. "In a nice pony-tail, perhaps!" Then he made his way to the table.

Did Tortoise say "Good Morning!" to anyone?

Did he ask how they had slept?

Did he take a second to bow his head and offer up a prayer of thanks?

No, he did not! Tortoise simply grabbed his bowl and sucked that porridge down in one long sickening slurp – muddy reeds and river bugs and all!

And then, of course, Tortoise was hungry for more. Not just some of the rest – but all of it!

So he made an excuse – "Oh dear, I've smeared a bit of river bug on my shell!" – and then ducked out into the kitchen as if to wipe it off. But once he got there, Tortoise went straight for the steaming hot porridge pot.

He would have gobbled it all down, right there and then, but he heard someone else coming towards the kitchen.

"Let me help you!" called his mother-in-law. "We don't want that river bug to stain!"

Tortoise panicked. He desperately wanted what was left of the porridge. But he was running out of time. So he dumped the porridge into his big floppy hat and, just as his mother-in-law came through the kitchen door, he plopped it back on his head!

203

"Oh, I see you've wiped it off already," said his mother-in-law. "And no stains at all. Excellent! Now come back to the table. There are a few things I need to ask you."

Tortoise staggered back to the table – his head boiling! He wanted to leave just as fast as he could. But his mother-in-law went on and on with her questions. How was his wife? How were the children? How were the next-door neighbours?

Finally, when Tortoise could stand the heat no longer, he jumped up from his seat and bolted for the door.

"Really must go!" he apologized. "I'll explain later. Sorry to eat and run."

Then Tortoise hurried out of the house, down the street, and ducked into an alley. Alone at last, he tore the hat off his head.

The porridge was still there, floating with reeds and river bugs. But something else was floating in there too – every last bit of Tortoise's beautiful black hair!

Tortoise looked in the hat and sighed.

His porridge was ruined.

His hair was gone.

If only he hadn't been so greedy.

And that, so they say, is why tortoises are bald to this very day.

Big Jack, Little Jack and the Bird

Big Jack and Little Jack were sad. Their little farm was failing and all their crops were gone. They were very, very poor.

"We've got no money!" sighed Big Jack.

"And no food, either!" added Little Jack.

So they went down to the river to catch some fish.

But even the fish weren't biting. So Big Jack and Little Jack went home empty-handed.

"We've caught no fish!" sighed Big Jack.

"No fish at all," added Little Jack. "I wish we'd caught just one – then we could have had some supper."

And that's when they saw a bird – a great big beautiful bird – sitting on the roof of their little rundown house.

"That's the biggest bird I've ever seen!" said Big Jack.

"And the most beautiful!" added Little Jack.

"That's very kind," said the bird. Then he flapped his wings and flew quickly out of sight.

"I believe that bird just spoke to us," said Big Jack.

"I believe you're right," said Little Jack.

And before they could say anything else, the bird returned, with a great big fish in his beak. "I heard your wish," said the bird. "I have very good hearing! And I will happily bring you a fish every day, if you like. Just as long as you let me sleep on your roof."

"That would be very helpful," said Big Jack.

"Very helpful indeed!" agreed Little Jack.

And so every day, for the next month, the great big beautiful bird brought

a great big
juicy fish to the house.
And Big Jack and Little Jack had
more than enough to eat.

But their neighbour, Nasty Jack, grew more and
more jealous with each passing day.

"Those boys do nothing!" he shouted at his wife. "And yet
that bird brings them a great big juicy fish every day. I wish I had
a bird like that. I'd hang onto him and never let him go." And that's
when Nasty Jack came up with his nasty plan.

"I'll steal that bird. That's what I'll do. I'll get my cousins to come and
help. And that bird and all those fish will be mine!"

So Nasty Jack called together all his nasty cousins. There was Sneaky
Jack and Creepy Jack. Angry Jack and Cranky Jack. Slappy Jack and
Snappy Jack. And Big Bad Ugly Bully Jack!

That very night, they crept through the hedge and up to Big Jack and
Little Jack's house. Then they climbed up onto the roof, where the great
big beautiful bird was sleeping.

Nasty Jack grabbed the bird by the leg, and the bird didn't even move.
He just opened his eyes and stared at Nasty Jack.

"Well then," said the bird, much to Nasty Jack's surprise, "it looks like
you've got your wish."

"Wish?" asked Nasty Jack. "What wish?"

"The wish you made to your wife," said the bird. "I have very good
hearing, you know. You said that if you ever got hold of a bird like me, you'd
never let him go. Now it's time for your wish to come true."

And with that, the great big beautiful bird flapped his wings and flew off
into the air. Nasty Jack tried to hold him down, but the bird was too strong,
and he lifted Nasty Jack up into the sky.

Nasty Jack did not like heights. But when he tried to let go of the bird –

he couldn't! His hands
were stuck fast. His wish had,
indeed, come true!

"Help me boys!" he called to his cousins. "Grab my leg and
we'll pull him down together!"

So Sneaky Jack grabbed Nasty Jack's leg, and Creepy Jack grabbed
Sneaky Jack's leg, and on and on it went. But as soon as the cousins
grabbed hold, they couldn't let go either! And soon there was a cursing,
grumbling, unhappy string of Jacks hanging from that bird's leg.

All their noise woke Big Jack and Little Jack, and they wandered sleepy-
eyed out of the house.

"Looks like a giant kite!" said Big Jack.

"A giant, noisy kite!" said Little Jack.

Then they both went back to bed.

The next morning, the great big beautiful bird was back on the roof.
He told Big Jack and Little Jack the whole story. And when they asked
what happened in the end, the bird just chuckled.

"I knew it would come sooner or later," he said. "Those nasty fellas got
tired of hanging on – so one of them wished that I'd just let them go. It was
a whisper – only a whisper. But I've got very good hearing, you know. So I
made his wish come true and dropped them in a swamp, many miles from
here. They won't be bothering us for a long while now. Anyone feel like
some fish?"

"I do!" said big Jack.

"Me too!" added Little Jack.

And the great big beautiful bird flapped his wings and flew off into
the sky.

How the Rabbit Lost Its Tail

Way back when the world was young, Rabbit had a long white tail!
   Sometimes it dragged on the ground behind him.
   Sometimes it stood straight up in the air.
   But all the time, it followed Rabbit wherever he went.
   One day, Rabbit wanted to visit an island, far across the sea. He curled up his tail like a long white spring, and sat there on the beach, bouncing and thinking. But no matter how long he bounced or how hard he thought, Rabbit could not find a way to get across the water.
   Then, a shark swam by. And suddenly, Rabbit had an idea. A sneaky idea, for Rabbit was quite a trickster.
   "Excuse me, Shark," he called. "I was just sitting here, bouncing and thinking – and I wondered – how many friends does a shark have?"
   "Friends?" Shark replied. "Hundreds and hundreds, I should think."
   "I'm surprised!" said Rabbit. "I always thought that sharks were quite fierce and lonely creatures."
   "A common mistake," Shark grinned, his bright white teeth gleaming in the sunlight.

208

"We're really very friendly, and only show our fierce side when something makes us angry. Let me show you."

And with that, Shark disappeared beneath the surface of the water. But, when he came up again, he was not alone. There were hundreds of sharks, grinning behind him, stretched out across the water, as far as Rabbit could see!

"I'm impressed!" said Rabbit. "So many friends! Would you mind if I counted them?"

"Of course not," grinned Shark. "Do what you like. It will only prove my point."

So Rabbit counted the sharks. He hopped onto their heads, one by one, counting them as he went.

He hopped on ten sharks and twenty sharks and thirty sharks.

He hopped on forty sharks and fifty sharks and sixty sharks.

He hopped on seventy sharks and eighty sharks and ninety sharks.

And when he had hopped onto a hundred sharks, Rabbit just kept hopping – until he had hopped on the heads of three hundred sharks.

And then, Rabbit hopped onto the island!

"So have I made my point?" asked Shark, who had been swimming alongside Rabbit, all the while.

"Absolutely!" Rabbit chuckled.

"Then what's so funny?" asked Shark.

Rabbit chuckled again. And then, because he found it impossible to keep a good trick to himself, he went on.

"Well, I really couldn't care less how many friends you have. I just needed a way to cross the sea!"

Then Rabbit turned to walk away from the beach, his long tail dancing behind him. But Shark did not turn away. No, he did not like being tricked and was angry at Rabbit for making a fool of him and his friends. So, as Rabbit turned, Shark leaped out of the water and, flashing his sharp teeth, bit off Rabbit's long white tail.

"Yowch!" cried Rabbit, running off into the woods – his tail now no more than a little white tuft of a thing.

But did that teach him a lesson? Did it cure Rabbit of his trickster ways? It did not.

For when it came time to leave the island, Rabbit sat on the beach again. And simply waited until he found a different kind of fish – a fish with more friends than teeth!

The Badger Teapot

The little badger bounced up and down the hillside. He rolled, he tumbled, he threw himself on the soft grass and stared into the sky. It was a beautiful spring day, and he was determined to enjoy every minute of it.

And then – sproing! – a hunter's noose, hidden in the grass, looped itself round his leg and held him fast. The little badger was trapped!

Ting-a-ling. Clang-clang. Plonkety-plonk. A poor tinker came tramping by, his pots and pans banging around on his back.

"Help me! Help me, please!" the badger cried. And the tinker felt so sorry for him that he untied the noose straightaway and set the badger free.

The badger bounced up and down again. "How can I ever repay you?" he asked the tinker. "I will do anything. Please tell me how."

"There is no need to repay me," smiled the tinker. "Run back to your home. Enjoy this lovely day. That is payment enough for me." And he tramped off again – Ting-a-ling, Clang-clang, Plonkety-plonk.

211

The badger, however, was determined to repay the tinker for his kindness.
And just before the tinker had walked out of sight, he had an idea. He wiggled
his badger nose. He shut his badger eyes. He shook his badger body. He wished
really hard. And he turned himself into a teapot! How he did it, he didn't quite
know, but there he was – a beautiful badger teapot, covered in delicate black
and white patterns, with a badger tail for a handle, and a badger nose for a
spout, and four porcelain badger feet.

Then he ran off after the tinker. And without the tinker knowing it, he leaped
onto the pile of pots and pans on the tinker's back and held tight – Ting-a-ling,
Clang-clang, Plonkety-plonk – all the way back to the tinker's house.

When the tinker unloaded his pots and pans, he was surprised to find the
teapot among them.

"Where did this come from?" asked his wife.

"I don't know," said the tinker. "But it's very nice, isn't it? Why don't you
make us some tea?"

And so the tinker's wife did. She set the teapot on the table. She boiled some
water. She poured it into the pot. And then – oh my! – the beautiful teapot

began to bounce around the room!

"Hot! Hot! Much too hot!" the teapot shrieked. So the tinker's wife picked it up and emptied it and called for her husband, the tinker.

"There's a ghost in this teapot!" she complained. "You must take it back to wherever you found it!"

"No! No!" the teapot cried. "I am not a ghost. I am the little badger you rescued on the hillside. I turned myself into a teapot to repay you."

"You're not much help, then," moaned the tinker's wife. "What good is a teapot that can't hold hot water?"

"I'll tell you what," said the teapot. "I'm still a badger at heart. I can tumble and balance and dance. Why not put on a little circus? And I will be your star!"

"I could make the curtains," offered the tinker's wife.

"And I could build a little stage," said the tinker. "Yes, why not! Thank you Badger Teapot."

So they sewed curtains and built a stage and put notices all around the village: "Come and see the Amazing Tumbling Teapot."

People were curious, of course, and paid good money to see this Tumbling Teapot. And they were not disappointed. The teapot did somersaults. The teapot did backflips. And, most impressive of all, the teapot walked across a tightrope, holding a bright red parasol in his snout – or rather – spout!

The people clapped. The people cheered. The people came from miles around. And soon the tinker was a very rich man indeed.

"You have repaid me more than I deserve," he said to the teapot, one day. "I think it is time you went back to your home."

"That is very kind," said the teapot. And with a wiggle and a wink and a shake and a wish, he turned himself back into a badger. How he did it, he didn't quite know, but when he had finished, the badger said goodbye and tumbled back to the hillside.

And the tinker and his wife and the badger, who was no longer a teapot, lived happily ever after.

213

The Kind of Hungry Lion

Once there was a kind of hungry lion, whose stomach growled softly, like a little lion cub.

The kind of hungry lion went to look for something to eat. He peeped around a boulder and saw a family of rock badgers having a picnic.

I'm not hungry enough to eat a whole rock badger, thought the kind of hungry lion. But half a badger would make a very nice snack.

Just then, his stomach growled again, louder this time, and the badgers looked his way.

"Look!" shouted a little brown rock badger. "A lion has come to our picnic!"

"Don't be shy," called the badger's wife. "Come along and join us!"

The kind of hungry lion didn't know what to think. But then his stomach growled a little louder. So he decided that he would join the badgers' picnic. And if he got tired of that, he could always picnic on the badgers!

The badgers brought the lion a deck chair and a little table. Then they poured him a glass of lemonade, with four ice cubes and a bendy straw!

Soon someone called, "Supper!" and all the badgers ran into a tall tent. By now, the kind of hungry lion had

214

become a hungry lion, and his stomach's growl was as loud as his own.

The rock badgers gave him the best seat and piled plates of pretty sandwiches in front of him. A toothpick, with a little sign, had been stuck into the top sandwich on each plate.

Everyone looked at the hungry lion. And the hungry lion looked at the little signs.

"Parsley" said the first sign. And the lion gagged. Even really hungry lions didn't eat parsley.

"Cress" said the second sign. And the lion gagged again. Even very hungry lions didn't eat cress.

There was only one sign left. The lion swallowed hard and then read it. "Clover" is what it said. And the lion thought he would cry.

What could he do? He was a hungry lion. But lions don't eat parsley and cress and clover. Lions eat meat! Like antelopes and buffaloes and… rock badgers.

But the rock badgers had been so kind to him. How could he eat them and spoil their lovely picnic?

215

And
that's when the hungry lion smelled something.
"What's that?" he asked.

The little brown rock badger sniffed the air. "It smells like something cooking," he said. "The jackals are having a picnic over the ridge. Perhaps the smell is coming from there."

The hungry lion stood up so fast he nearly poked his head through the top of the tent. "I'm very sorry," he apologized. "I have to go now. Thank you for a lovely afternoon." And with that, the hungry lion dashed off after that wonderful smell. He was a very hungry lion now, and his stomach was roaring as only a lion's stomach can.

What could they be cooking? he wondered. Antelope? Camel? Elephant stew? And then he reached the jackals' picnic and just stood and stared at the fattest, juiciest ox he had ever seen! Two jackals were turning it on a spit and splashing it with barbecue sauce.

"Excuse me," asked the very hungry lion. "Could I join you for dinner?"
The jackals didn't smile or say "Hello". They didn't even look at him.
"Get in the queue!" barked one of the jackals. "Over by the table."

The lion took his roaring stomach over to the end of the queue. The jackals were pushing and shoving one another, and, before he knew it, the very hungry lion was being pushed and shoved too. There were jackal elbows in his back and jackal knees up his nose, but at last he crawled out of that jumble with a knife and a fork and a plate – and a thick, juicy ox steak!

He sat down at the table, but before he could pick up his knife, an old grey jackal spat and hollered, "That's MY seat! I've been coming to jackal picnics for fifty years, and I ALWAYS sit there!"

The very hungry lion picked up his plate and found himself between two angry lady jackals. They were snapping and snarling and waving their handbags and, before the lion could move, one of the handbags slammed against his plate and sent it flying. And the very hungry lion watched his steak fall flat onto the ground!

The lion bent down and picked up his steak. His dinner was now a brown muddy mess. "You know what you are?" he roared. "You're nothing but a bunch of ANIMALS!" Then he stomped out of the clearing and back over the ridge.

Now a very, very hungry lion, he stomped right back to the badgers' picnic, straight into their big tent.

And then there was a roar, a roar so loud and fierce that all the other animals stopped their picnics to listen. The roar was followed by the sound of running feet, overturned tables and broken plates. And, finally, everything went quiet.

The other animals spent a sad moment thinking about the poor rock badgers and how they had ended up as part of the lion's dinner.

Meanwhile, inside the tent, the very full and happy lion leaned back in his chair and licked the tips of his claws.

"I've never heard a stomach growl so loudly in all my life," said the little brown rock badger. "I'm just glad we had more sandwiches. But I'm sorry we made such a noise and fuss getting it all together."

"Just as long as our guest enjoyed himself," smiled the badger's wife. "And by the looks of him, I'd say he did. Can we get you anything else?" she asked the lion.

The lion patted his quiet tummy. "Yes please," he smiled. "I think I've got room for just one more of those clover sandwiches."

The Big, Soft, Fluffy Bed

Granny put Danny to bed – in her big, soft, fluffy bed.

But when she closed the door behind her – closed it ever so slowly and ever so gently – the hinge on the door went Squeeeek!

And Danny woke up with a cry!

"Oh dear," said Granny, "I know what we'll do. We'll let the kitten sleep with you, just this once. And she can keep you company!"

So Granny put Danny to bed again – in her big, soft, fluffy bed.

With the kitten curled up at his feet.

But when she closed the door – closed it ever so slowly and ever so gently – the hinge on the door went Squeeeek!

Danny woke up with a cry!

And the kitten jumped up with a "Miaow!"

"Oh dear," said Granny, "I know what we'll do. We'll let the dog sleep with you, just this once. He can keep you company!"

So Granny put Danny to bed again – in her big, soft, fluffy bed.

With the kitten curled up at his feet.

And the dog stretched out beside him.

But when she closed the door – closed it ever so slowly and ever so gently – the hinge on the door went Squeeeek!

Danny woke up with a cry!

The kitten jumped up with a "Miaow!"

And the dog leaped up with a "Woof!"

"Oh dear," said Granny, "I know what we'll do. We'll let the pig sleep with you, just this once. She can keep you company!"

So Granny put Danny to bed again – in her big, soft, fluffy bed.

With the kitten curled up at his feet.

And the dog stretched out beside him.

And the pig right next to his pillow.

But when she closed the door – closed it ever so slowly and ever so gently – the hinge on the door went Squeeek!

Danny woke up with a cry!

The kitten jumped up with a "Miaow!"

The dog leaped up with a "Woof!"

And the pig rolled over with an "Oink!"

"Oh dear," said Granny, "I know what we'll do. We'll let the pony sleep with you, just this once, and he can keep you company!"

So Granny put Danny to bed again – in her big, soft, fluffy bed.

With the kitten curled up at his feet.

And the dog stretched out beside him.

And the pig right next to his pillow.

And the pony squeezed between them all!

But when she closed the door – closed it ever so slowly and ever so gently – the hinge on the door went Squeeeek!

Danny woke up with a cry!

The kitten jumped up with a "Miaow!"

The dog leaped up with a "Woof!"

The pig rolled over with an "Oink!"

The pony bounced up and down with a "Neigh!"
And the big, soft, fluffy bed fell down with a crash.
"Oh dear," said Granny, "this will never do!"
So she shooed the kitten back into the kitchen.
Walked the dog out into the yard.
Persuaded the pig to go back to her pigsty.
And led the pony to the barn.
Then Granny mended the big, soft, fluffy bed.
She looked at the door.
She looked at the rusty hinge.
And then she went out to the shed and came back with a little can of oil.
Granny squirted the oil on the hinge, then one last time, she put Danny
to bed – in the big, soft, fluffy bed.
And when she closed the door – closed it ever so slowly and ever so gently
– the hinge on the door… made no sound at all!
And Danny fell fast asleep.

The Peanut Boy

Henry and his dad were going fishing.

They packed their tackle and their bait. They slung their fishing rods over their shoulders. But just as they were about to leave for the river, Henry's mum asked Henry's dad to step into the kitchen.

Henry's mum and Henry's dad talked and talked and talked.

Henry waited and waited.

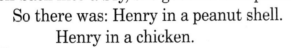

And when he got tired of waiting, he decided to do something just a little more interesting. He decided to turn himself into a peanut!

How he did it, nobody knew.

Where he learned it was a mystery.

But it was a talent – no question about that.

So Henry shut his eyes. Henry scrunched up his face. And, in a flash, Henry was a peanut, tucked up in a peanut shell.

He sat there for a while, all cosy and peanut-like. And then a chicken came clucking by. She saw the peanut lying on the ground, and, before Henry could turn himself back into a boy, she gobbled that peanut up.

So there was: Henry in a peanut shell.

Henry in a chicken.

And Henry's mum and Henry's dad just talking in the kitchen.

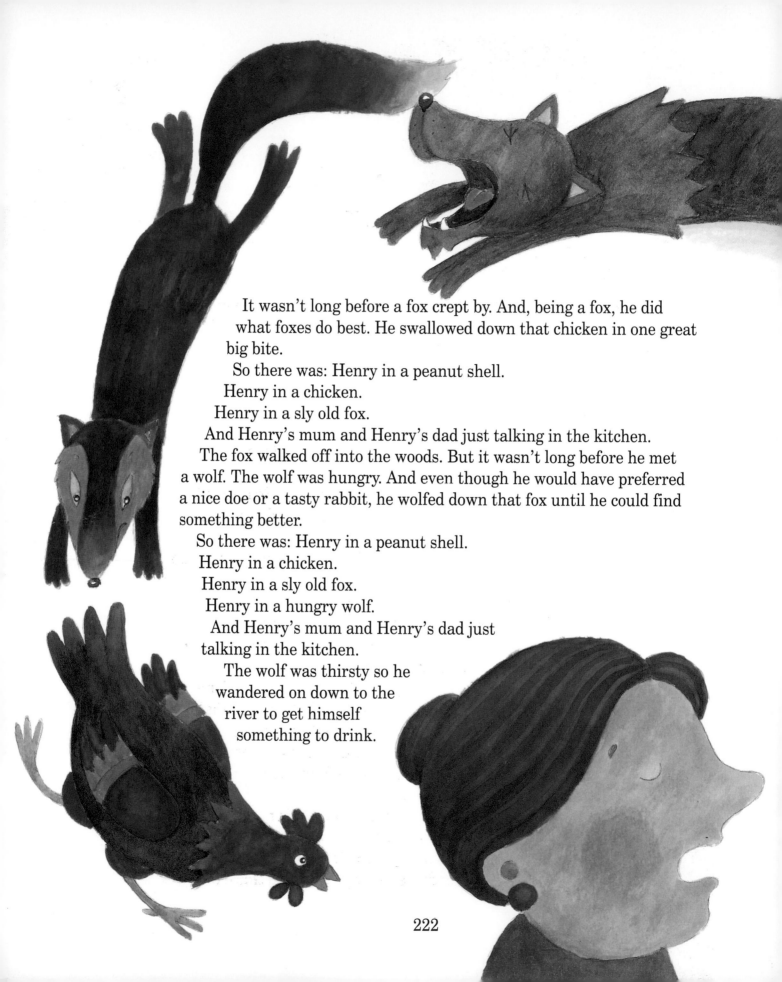

It wasn't long before a fox crept by. And, being a fox, he did what foxes do best. He swallowed down that chicken in one great big bite.

So there was: Henry in a peanut shell.

Henry in a chicken.

Henry in a sly old fox.

And Henry's mum and Henry's dad just talking in the kitchen.

The fox walked off into the woods. But it wasn't long before he met a wolf. The wolf was hungry. And even though he would have preferred a nice doe or a tasty rabbit, he wolfed down that fox until he could find something better.

So there was: Henry in a peanut shell.

Henry in a chicken.

Henry in a sly old fox.

Henry in a hungry wolf.

And Henry's mum and Henry's dad just talking in the kitchen.

The wolf was thirsty so he wandered on down to the river to get himself something to drink.

But when he dipped his tongue into the water, up sprang the biggest fish he had ever seen and gulped him down between its big, fat, fishy lips!

So there was: Henry in a peanut shell.

Henry in a chicken.

Henry in a sly old fox.

Henry in a hungry wolf.

Henry in a great big fish.

And Henry's mum and Henry's dad just talking in the kitchen.

At last the talking stopped.

Henry's mum had had her say. And Henry's dad had too. So he went out looking for Henry. His tackle and his bait and his fishing rod were right outside the kitchen door. But Henry was gone.

Probably tired of waiting, thought Henry's dad. So he went down to the river, alone.

He put the bait on his hook.

He tossed the line into the river.

And what took hold of that line was the biggest fish he had ever seen.

Henry's dad pulled and pulled and pulled. And, finally, he pulled that big fish right up onto the shore.

He reached his hand into the fish's mouth to fetch his hook – and out popped the wolf!

The wolf opened his mouth to howl – and out popped the fox!

The fox opened his mouth to catch his breath – and out popped the chicken!

223

The chicken sneezed – and out popped the peanut!

And as soon as Henry's dad saw the peanut, he nodded his head and he grinned. You see, he knew all about Henry's special talent. So he did what he always did when Henry hid himself in a peanut.

He picked up the peanut, tossed it in the air and said, as loudly as he could, "I think it's time to make some peanut butter!"

And, as soon as Henry heard that, he turned himself into a boy again. "I'm feeling a little hungry," said Henry's dad.

"Me too," said Henry.

So they picked up the fish and carried it home. And, as they fried it up in their very biggest pan, Henry told his mum and dad about everything that had happened:

Henry in a peanut shell.

Henry in a chicken.

Henry in a sly old fox.

Henry in a hungry wolf.

Henry in a great big fish.

Henry safe back home again.

And Henry's mum and Henry's dad just listening in the kitchen.

The Wonderful Bird

The three sisters worked hard in the fields. They planted and weeded and helped with the harvest, even though they were very young. But what else could they do? Their parents were dead. They were poor and hungry, and their greedy uncle would do nothing to help them.

One afternoon, as they were finishing their work, the three sisters stumbled across a wounded little bird. She fluttered and flapped and flopped about on the ground. They were sad to see her like this so they they picked her up carefully and carried her home. Then they made a little bird cage out of sticks and, day by day, nursed her back to health.

"Kekeko. Kekeko." That was the sound the little bird made when she was well again. So that's what the sisters named her – Kekeko.

One evening, just as the sisters were preparing for bed, Kekeko did something that surprised them. She did not stick her head under her wing. She did not say, "Kekeko." No, she looked straight at the sisters and she spoke!

"Let me sleep in your biggest basket tonight," chirped Kekeko. "And I will lay some food for you."

The three sisters stared at the bird. They were so shocked to hear her speak that they did just what she asked. But the next morning, when they awoke,

225

they were even more surprised. For Kekeko was back in her cage, and the basket was full of cooked fish and warm rice!

"See!" cried Kekeko. "I have laid for you! Put me in the basket again tonight, and I will do the same."

The hungry sisters did not stop to wonder how a bird could lay such food. They just gobbled down the fish and rice. They had never eaten so much! That night, Kekeko filled the basket again. And again and again, each night that followed.

Soon, Kekeko was laying so much fish and rice that the girls could not finish it.

"Would it be possible for you to lay uncooked rice instead?" asked the most sensible sister, at last. "That way we could store it, and perhaps pass it on to some of our poorer neighbours."

Kekeko was happy to oblige. She laid so much rice, in fact, that the girls had enough for themselves and all their poor friends. Word of their good fortune spread across the village. And that is when their greedy uncle came to visit.

"I understand you have a wonderful bird!" he said. "And that she lays you more rice than you can use. Would you mind if I took her home with me for a day or two?"

The sisters looked at one another. This was a hard decision. Their uncle had never shown them any kindness. But did that mean that they should refuse to be kind to him?

In the end, they agreed to let him borrow her. "We have more than enough to eat," they said. "We are happy to share our good fortune with you."

So the greedy uncle put Kekeko in her cage and carried her off to his house.

One day passed. And a second. And a third. The girls still had plenty to eat, but they were missing their little friend very much now. So they went to their uncle's house and knocked on his door.

"Excuse us," they said, "but could we have Kekeko back now?"

"I don't think so," said the greedy uncle.

"Why?" asked one of the sisters. "Because you want her to lay more rice?"

"No," the uncle scowled. "Because I have eaten her!"

At once, the three sisters burst into tears.

"Stop your blubbering!" the uncle shouted. "The silly bird deserved it! I put her in a basket two nights in a row – the biggest basket I could find. And did she give me any rice? Not a grain. All she did was chirp on and on about how I had neglected you. So I put an end to her chirping and had her for my breakfast. And a tiny breakfast it was, at that!"

Then the greedy uncle went into the kitchen, scooped up Kekeko's bones and gave them to the girls, along with her little birdcage.

"Here," he sneered. "See for yourselves. This is all that's left!"

The three sisters trudged home, weeping as they went. They had no thought for the future or for what they would do when the rice ran out. They thought only about poor little Kekeko.

So when they returned home, the first thing they did was to bury her. They put the bones in the bird cage. They put the cage in a hole. Then they covered the hole with dirt and laid the basket on the top. And, weeping still, they went to bed.

When they woke the next
morning, the three sisters went into the garden
to look at Kekeko's grave. But the grave was gone!
In its place stood a little tree, with broad leafy branches. And,
hanging on the branches, were silver rings and golden necklaces
and more shiny treasures than the girls had ever seen. The three
sisters would never be poor again!

But best of all, when the wind blew through the branches,
there came a sound – "Kekeko. Kekeko." And the sisters
knew that their little friend was with them still.

The Cat, the Mice and the Cheese

Once upon a time, there were two little mice who stumbled across one great big chunk of cheese.

"It's mine!" said the grey mouse. "I saw it first!"

"Yours?" cried the brown mouse. "I beg to differ, but I think it's mine!"

And they squeaked and scratched and squabbled for an hour or more.

"This is getting us nowhere," sighed the grey mouse, at last. "Why don't we just split it?"

"And I suppose you'll be the one who does the splitting," said the brown mouse. "I can see what you're up to."

"Well, I wouldn't want you to do it," sneered the grey mouse. "You'd be sure to cut yourself the bigger piece."

Suddenly, another voice joined the conversation. "Perhaps I can be of some help."

And when the mice turned around, there appeared a huge ginger cat!

229

There was no time to run. Nowhere to hide. So the mice just stood there, shivering with fear.

"There's nothing to be afraid of," grinned the cat. "I am here to help. You may not believe this, but I like a bit of cheese, myself, from time to time. So I understand your problem perfectly. Why not let *me* divide the cheese for you?"

The mice looked at each another. It seemed a reasonable solution. And, besides, they didn't have much choice.

"All right," said the grey mouse.

"As long as you're fair," added the brown mouse.

And the cat grinned again. Then he reached out one sharp claw and cut the cheese in two.

But as soon as he'd finished, it was clear that one piece was bigger than the other.

"The big piece is mine!" squeaked the grey mouse.

"Oh no it isn't!" squeaked the brown mouse in reply. And the argument started up again.

"I'm terribly sorry!" apologized the cat. "It seems that I have made things even worse. Here, let me put it right."

And he shaved a bit off the bigger piece – and popped it into his mouth!

"Mmm," said the cat. "Very nice. Very nice, indeed!"

"But it's still not right!" complained the grey mouse. "You shaved off too much. Now the other piece is bigger!"

"MY piece, you mean!" squeaked the brown mouse. "You didn't want it! Remember?"

"I want it now that it's bigger!" cried the grey mouse.

And the cat had to interrupt again.

"Now, now," he purred. "This is easily fixed." And again he shaved a bit off the bigger piece and popped it into his mouth!

"Creamy!" he mewed. "So thick and so rich."

But the mice were still not happy – not happy at all. For now the other piece was bigger again.

On and on went the arguing. And so did the shaving and the eating and the purring as, bit by bit, the cat gobbled up the cheese. Finally, there was nothing left, but one last bite.

"Wait a minute!" cried the grey mouse. "The cheese is almost gone!"

"That's right," cried the brown mouse. "So that last little piece is mine!"

"Oh no it's not!" squeaked the grey mouse.

And the cat just grinned again.

"I see what you mean," he said. "It's only a little piece, isn't it? Hardly worth fighting over."

And with that, he speared the cheese with his claw and popped it into his mouth!

The grey mouse and the brown mouse both gasped in horror!

"You've eaten it all!" they cried. "And we've had nothing!"

"Nothing but a good argument," said the cat. "And you might have had so much more, if only you had been a little less greedy and tried a little harder to get along."

"It's not fair!" squeaked the grey mouse. "You've cheated us."

"Careful," growled the cat. "I only did what I promised. If I were you, I'd be grateful that the cheese was not the only thing I gobbled down!"

Then he cleaned his claws and licked his lips and padded away.

And the grey mouse and the brown mouse trudged sadly home.

The Goats and the Hyena

Once upon a time, on a high and grassy hill, there lived three goats.

Siksik was the biggest.

Mikmik was almost as big.

And the smallest was Jureybon.

One day, the three goats went for a walk – through the rocky passes to a field on the next hill. They grazed all day and, as the sun began to set, they set off for home.

Siksik led the way – for he was the biggest.

Mikmik followed close behind – for he was almost as big.

And little Jureybon straggled far behind – for he was the smallest.

They squeezed past huge boulders and leaped over deep ravines. But as Siksik turned the very last corner, he found himself face to face with a very big and very hungry hyena!

"I have three questions for you, goat!" growled the hyena.

"Ask away, sir," Siksik trembled.

"What are those points on your head?" the hyena asked.

"They are my horns, sir," Siksik trembled.

"What is that patch on your back?"

"It is my woolly coat, sir."

"Then why are you shivering?" the hyena roared.

"Because I am afraid that you will eat me, sir," cried Siksik.

232

"For my dinner, I think!" the hyena drooled. Then, with one blow of his paw, he knocked Siksik down cold.

And, not a second later, Mikmik turned the corner.

"I have three questions for you, goat!" growled the hyena.

"Ask away, sir," Mikmik trembled.

"What are those points on your head?" the hyena asked.

"They are my horns, sir," Mikmik trembled.

"What is that patch on your back?"

"It is my woolly coat, sir."

"Then why are you shivering?" the hyena roared.

"Because I am afraid that you will eat me, sir," cried Mikmik.

"For my breakfast, I think!" the hyena drooled. And, with one blow of his paw, he knocked Mikmik out as well.

If Jureybon had been bigger, if Jureybon had been faster, if Jureybon had not been straggling behind, he too might have turned the corner a second later.

But he was the smallest goat, and the slowest – so he had time to come up with a plan!

He hid around the corner, so that the hyena could not see him. Then he called out in the deepest and angriest voice he could muster: "I have three questions for you, hyena!"

The hyena was confused. This was his line!

"Ask away, sir," the hyena growled.

"What are these points on my head?" asked Jureybon.

The hyena was even more confused. "Your horns?" he guessed.

"No, you fool!" roared Jureybon. "These are my two sharp swords!"

"Second question. What is this patch on my back?" Jureybon continued.

The hyena did not like this one bit. "Your woolly coat?" he trembled.

"Coat?" howled Jureybon. "Don't be ridiculous. This is my mighty shield!"

Shield? wondered the hyena. Swords? And he grew more nervous still.

"And finally!" growled Jureybon. "One last question. Why am I shivering?"

"Because you are afraid, sir?" the hyena shivered back.

"Because I am trembling with rage!!" roared Jureybon. "And cannot wait to come round this corner and knock you out!"

The hyena couldn't wait either – to get away! He forgot all about his breakfast and his dinner and ran all the way back to his cave.

Then Jureybon danced happily round the corner. He woke up Siksik. He woke up Mikmik. And the three goats went back to their high and grassy hill.

The Clever Crows

Big Crow and Little Crow were thirsty.

It had not rained for months. The world was like a desert. Everything was dry.

Then Big Crow spotted a bottle – a clear glass bottle – in a dark corner of a shady courtyard. And in the bottom of the bottle there was water! Not much water, but enough for both of them to have a drink.

Little Crow stuck his beak into the bottle. And, as soon as he did, he began to cry.

"The water's too far down!" he wept. "We'll never reach it."

"And if we tip the bottle over," sighed Big Crow in reply, "the water will soak into the dry ground before we have a chance to drink it."

But then Big Crow spotted a pebble – a shiny black pebble – in the middle of the courtyard. And Big Crow had an idea.

He hopped into the middle of the courtyard, picked up the pebble and hopped back into the shady corner.

Then he winked and said to Little Crow, "Watch this!"

With the pebble in his beak, he put his beak in the bottle. He dropped the pebble in the water, and the water rose higher!

Little Crow peered into the bottle.

"There's one pebble down there," he said. "But the water is still too low for me to reach."

"Then we will have to put in more," said Big Crow. And he picked up a silver pebble, and a bright white one too.

And, with the pebbles in his beak, he put his beak in the bottle. He dropped the pebbles in the water, and the water rose higher!

"One pebble. And two more pebbles. That makes three pebbles," said Little Crow. "And that's a lot better. But the water is still too low."

"Then we will add some more," said Big Crow. And he found a brown pebble and a green pebble and a white pebble.

And, with the pebbles in his beak, he put his beak in the bottle. He dropped the pebbles in the water, and the water rose higher!

"Three more pebbles," said Little Crow. "That makes six altogether. But the water is still too low. Can I drop the pebbles in this time?"

"Be my guest!" said Big Crow.

So Little Crow (who was very thirsty by now) found four pebbles – a red one, a purple one, a yellow one and a blue one.

And, with the pebbles in his beak, he put his beak in the bottle. He dropped the pebbles in the water, and the water rose higher!

"Six pebbles and four pebbles. That makes ten pebbles now!" said Big Crow. "I think we've finally done it!"

And so they had. For when Little Crow stuck his beak into the bottle, he could finally reach the water!

So Little Crow had a drink. And Big Crow did too. And then they flew away, leaving one glass bottle and ten shiny pebbles.

The Monkeys and the Mangoes

Once upon a time, at the edge of a mighty river, a little monkey found a mango tree.

He munched on the mango and – Mmm! – it was amazing. Sweet and juicy and more delicious than anything he had ever tasted.

The little monkey crossed the river and took the mango to the Monkey King. And when the Monkey King munched on the mango – Mmm! – he thought it was amazing too.

So the Monkey King, along with many more monkeys, made his way across the river to the mango tree.

The monkeys picked mangoes all morning and all afternoon, until it was night. Then they curled up in the branches of the mango tree and fell fast asleep. They had managed to eat many mangoes, but there were many more mangoes left. As they slept, one of those mangoes dropped from its branch into the mighty river, and floated downstream to the kingdom of men.

The next morning, as the King of Men was bathing in the river, the mango floated by. The king had never seen a mango before, but he thought it looked quite tasty. So he picked it up and handed it to one of his servants.

"Eat this!" he commanded. "Is it good? Is it bad? Is it poison? I need to know!"

So the servant munched on the mango and – Mmm! – it was amazing!

"The fruit is sweet and juicy!" he told the king. "More delicious than anything I have ever eaten!"

So the King of Men took a bite and – Mmm! – he thought it was amazing too!

"Call my soldiers!" he commanded. "We must travel up river and find more of this amazing fruit."

So the King of Men, his servants and his soldiers made their way to the mango tree. When the Monkey King saw them coming, he led the rest of the monkeys into the highest branches of the mango tree and told them to keep very, very still.

The servants picked mangoes all morning and all afternoon, and, just as it was turning dark, one of the soldiers spotted the tail of the little monkey, hanging down from the highest branch.

When he told the King of Men, the king just grinned.

"Roast monkey will go very nicely with this fruit," he said. "Take your bows and shoot the monkey down!"

Soon, arrows began to sail through the branches of the mango tree. The Monkey King knew that there was

only one thing to do. He was the biggest monkey of them all, so he leaped from the branches of the mango tree, across the mighty river, to a tree on the other side. Then he tied a long vine around one of his legs and leaped back across the river. He hoped to make a vine bridge so the monkeys could escape. But the vine was too short, and he could only make the bridge reach by stretching out his own body and holding onto the nearest mango branch.

So the Monkey King, himself, was now part of the bridge and he called for the monkeys to climb across his back to the other side.

"There are too many of us!" cried the little monkey. "We will break your back!"

"Just do as I say!" commanded the Monkey King.

So with the arrows flying all around, the monkeys climbed across their king's back to the safety of the farther shore.

The King of Men watched, amazed. Then he ordered his soldiers to put down their bows.

"Fetch me that monkey!" he commanded, pointing to the Monkey King. But, by the time the soldiers carried him down, the Monkey King was almost dead. For, as the little monkey had worried, the weight of the rest of the monkeys had broken his back.

The King of Men held the Monkey King in his arms and asked him one simple question: "Why? Why did you do it?"

The Monkey King's answer was more simple still.

"To save my people," he whispered. "For they are more important to me than any mango. More important than anything at all."

Then the Monkey King closed his eyes and died.

The King of Men looked at his own people – at his servants and at his soldiers. Then he ordered them to leave the mangoes and to follow him back to the kingdom of men. And there, in his own palace, the King of Men built a beautiful tomb for the Monkey King, so that he would never forget how a true king should act.

Sharing stories with a crowd

Storytelling was never meant to be a one-way street. At its best, it is a kind of dialogue, something that happens between a storyteller and their listeners. One way to encourage this in a larger group is to give your audience specific ways to participate in the story. Here are my suggestions for how to get groups of children (or adults) more involved in the stories from *The Lion Storyteller Awesome Book of Stories*. It's all very simple, although sometimes you may need to spend a while teaching people how to say their lines.

Some of these suggestions will also work when you're sharing the stories with only one or two children (although you may not want to make bedtime reading too exciting). They may even spark off other storytelling ideas of your own.

The main thing is to have fun with the storytelling and if an idea doesn't work, try something else instead. Enjoy yourself – and your listeners will enjoy themselves too.

The Mouse and the Lion

Hold your hands in front of your face, palms down (as if you're about to play the piano), then wiggle your fingers and go "Squeakity, squeakity, squeakity". Get everyone to do this with you whenever the little mouse skitters left and right and off to his destination. They might also pretend to gnaw and nibble and chew when the mouse frees the lion.

Silly Jack

Before I start this story, I borrow the props from the audience and line them up on the floor in front of me. I borrow a coin (for the coin!), a cup or a mug or a water bottle (for the jug), a jumper (for the cat), a shoe with a shoelace (for the lamb), and then ask for two volunteers – one to play the donkey (usually a boy), and one to play the most beautiful girl in the village (usually a girl!). The donkey has to go "hee-haw" when the donkey is mentioned and the girl has to go "Oo-la-la" when the beautiful girl is mentioned.

At the appropriate times, I flip the coin in the air and drop it, pretend to pour milk from the jug into my pocket, hold the jumper on my head and then toss it in the air (usually back to its owner), drag the shoe across the floor, and carry the donkey, piggy-back style on my back. (Make sure there is another adult in the room if you do this because of Child Protection issues.)

The Girl Who Played With the Stars

This is a story in which everyone can do everything (particularly important with under sixes) or you can divide the audience into smaller groups and give each group one of the actions.

Everything can become quite active, so why not ask your audience to stand up? They can pretend to swim with the girl, dance with the fairies (and perhaps even hum a little dancing tune), ride on the back of Four Feet (mime riding motion and make a neighing or clop-clopping sound), splash-splash on the back of No Feet At All, pretend to climb onto the backs of the gulls (make a gull crying sound at each step) and then dance again with the clouds.

Three Months' Night

Divide your group in half. One group plays the chipmunk, the other the bear. Teach the first half to use a squeaky little voice and say the chipmunk's line, "One day, one night." Teach the other half to say the bear's line, "Three months' day, three months' night" in a deep growly voice. Lead them to join in when the animals make their suggestions during the contest. If you do it in a rhythmic way, everyone will just keep going. You can get them to become louder and louder, then stop them and then tell them about the bear's mistake. You might also want to ask everyone to howl with the coyote, or maybe just play the coyote yourself.

Arion and the Dolphin

Divide your group into three parts. The first group shouts "Bang!" The second group shouts "Boom!" And the last group cries "Aaaah!" Bring them in at the places in the story where people drop things at the sound of Arion's harp. If you do the "Aaah" right, it will also work for the gulls' cry and the trembling sailors!

Rabbit and Tiger Save the World

Divide your group into two parts: Tiger and Rabbit. The Tigers roar with you after the first three descriptions and perhaps say "Doh" (like Homer Simpson) at the end of the fourth.

The Rabbits shrink away and cower at the end of the first description, give a happy little smile at the end of the second, and put their hands to their heads (like bunny ears) at the third.

When Tiger chases Rabbit, everyone can run on the spot. And when Rabbit throws his arms against the boulder, the Rabbits throw their arms out wide to mime this. Then, when Tiger is tricked, the other group should throw their arms out wide as well.

The Shepherd and the Clever Princess

Divide your group into three and teach each one an animal sound: the chirping sparrow, the scratching squirrel, and the cawing crow. Then bring each group in to the story at the appropriate point. With younger groups (say, six and under), you might want everyone to make all the sounds.

With older groups, you might also want to pick three volunteers to play the failed suitors: someone "wise" (give him some clever thing to say), someone "strong" (ask him to show his muscles), someone "handsome" (maybe says "hey, good lookin'!").

Tortoise Brings Food

Everyone can play the animals with you. Hold your arms around your head for the lion's mane. Put your hands to the side of your head for the rabbit's ears. Hold an arm in front of your face for the elephant's trunk. And pull the neck of your top up under your nose (if you're able to) for the turtle. Do this whenever the appropriate animals appear in the story, particularly when they run up and down the mountain. When they crash into the anthill, everyone shakes their heads and looks stunned. You might also want everyone to repeat "Uwungelema" along with the old man, in a shaky old man's voice.

Polly and the Frog

Divide your audience into three or four groups. Teach everyone to go "bar-durp" like the frog. Each group could do the "bar-durp" in a slightly different way – high, low, silly, loud and soft. Bring in a group whenever you get to a "bar-durp" in the story. It will keep everyone watching and waiting for when it's their turn!

Rabbit and Tiger Go Fishing

Everyone plays Tiger. They growl when he growls in the story and roar when he roars.

The Mouse Deer's Wisdom

Borrow five coins from your audience (bring along five of your own as a reserve). Count them out whenever the Mouse Deer does this in the story. Dropping them on a hard surface works best to get that "ringing" effect, so if the floor isn't hard, you might want to drop them onto a plate.

The Four Friends

Standing on the spot, show your audience how to fly with the raven, chew with the rat, swim and walk slowly with the turtle, and run or strain against the net with the goat. Then you can either divide them into four groups (with everyone doing the actions simultaneously as the rescue progresses) or get everyone to do the actions in order. Repeat them in the second rescue.

The Brave Bull Calf

Have your audience play the parts of the tiger, the leopard, and the dragon – growling and clawing the air in the case of the first two, and roaring and shaking their heads for the dragon.

Tiger Gets Stuck

Half the group plays the Rabbit and repeats "Hey, Hidey-hole. Ho, Hidey-hole. Are you happy, Hidey-hole?" after you. The other half plays Tiger. They pretend to squeeze into the hidey-hole and then repeat Tiger's silly hidey-hole answer.

The Clever Mouse

Everyone can follow the mouse-like actions from "The Mouse and the Lion". Lead them in going "Squeakity, squeakity, squeakity" every time the mouse climbs or scampers or scurries around Cadog's desk. And when he runs off with the thread tied around his leg, as well!

The Amazing Pine Cone

You'll need a few props for one: a small pile of coins (borrow these from the crowd if you like); a long piece of cloth (or a jumper, borrowed again from your audience); and a pine cone (you will probably need to bring this yourself) that you keep hidden until it appears in the story. Use these props as appropriate during your storytelling.

Half the group plays the mayor's wife and repeats "Go away!" after you. The rest play the poor woman and repeat "How can I help you?" after you. And at the end of the story, lead the mayor's wife half in sneezing for as long as you are able!

The Very Strong Sparrow

Everyone can join in the animal sounds when they appear in the story: "Ka-thoom, Kathoom" for the elephant, "Ker-splash, Ker-splash" for the crocodile, and "Too-tweet, Too-tweet" for the baby birds. If you prefer, you can also have a smaller group for each sound.

Simple John

Divide your audience into three parts – one for the eldest brother, one for the second brother, and one for Simple John.

When the brothers find the ants, the first group repeats the eldest brother's line "Ants are nasty!" after you. The second group repeats the second brother's line, "And they're good for nothing but treading on". Lastly, using a silly voice, the third group repeats Simple John's lines, sentence by sentence after you with particular emphasis on his description of the ants.

Use this pattern when they meet the ducks and the bees too.

The Selfish Sand Frog

Ask your audience to make noisy drinking sounds when Frog drinks up the water-hole, the billabong and the lake.

The Mouse's Bride

Your group plays the moon, the cloud, the wind and the mountain. When the mice meet the moon, they hold their arms in a crescent shape and go "Moooon!" in a mysterious voice. When they meet the cloud, they bounce up and down and go "Puffy!" in a high voice. When they meet the wind, they make a "Whooo" sound and wave their arms about. And when they meet the mountain, they hold their arms in an inverted V and in a deep voice say, "MOUNTAIN!" This also works well with a group for each "character".

The Big Wave

Your audience can be the people in the village, playing their parts at the right moment in the story. Divide them into little groups – old men and young men and mothers and grandmothers and babies and boys and girls – who say "Hello!" in appropriate voices (except for the babies, who go "Waaa!"). They can then make "party" noises. And finally they can pound their feet on the floor as they run up the hill.

Alternatively, they play the wave – pounding their feet on the floor, lightly at first when the old man sees the wave, and then more and more loudly as it rushes towards the village and hits it with a crash.

Tiger and the Storm

Divide your audience into three groups – one to pound their feet on the floor like Mrs Rabbit, one to hoot like Owl, and one to howl like Dog. Bring them in like Rabbit does and out again, one by one, as the "storm" subsides.

The Knee-High Man

Have your audience pretend to be the Knee-High Man. Have them gobble up oats and run in place like the horse, chew grass and bellow like the bull, and then climb up the tree to sit with the owl.

The Clever Baker

Divide your group into four parts and bring them in at the appropriate times, making as much noise as possible. The "bowl and spoon" make a stirring motion and go "clackety-clackety-clack". The cat goes "Yow! Yow! Yow!" The dog goes "Woof! Woof! Woof!" And the last group yells "Wah! Wah! Wah!" with the baby. As an alternative, when I am in schools, I will often have the boys play the bowl and spoon, the girls play the cat, the women teachers play the dog, and the men teachers (there are usually only one or two) play the baby. It gets a good laugh!

How the Kangaroo Got Its Tail

Everyone jumps up and down like the kangaroo children – both when they are introduced and later when the bandicoot comes after them. You could also lead them in making a tug-of-war pulling motion when they struggle with the bandicoot.

The Greedy Farmer

Choose someone who can sing to play the Fairy of the Lake. Teach them a simple tune (a commonly known traditional tune is best, but a popular contemporary song can be really funny). Everyone else (the cows) puts their fingers like horns at the side of their heads.

When the fairy sings in the story, the fairy-person sings their tune and everyone else sways and moos and pretend to follows wherever she or he leads.

The Generous Bird

Everyone walks like the bird in the story as he makes his way from place to place – knees jerking, head bobbing and hands dragging behind like his tail.

Tiger Eats a Monkey

Half the group plays the monkeys, screeching and hooting whenever they do in the story. The other half plays Tiger, making a tossing motion as he throws the monkey into the air, and a spitting, hissing, howling commotion when he swallows the tamarind fruit.

Lazy Tom

Ask everyone to make a hammering motion and the little click-clacking sound of the leprechaun at work. Do this at the beginning while Tom looks for the leprechaun – until the moment he grabs him – and also at the end. Lead Tom among the seated children, stop at one of them, and ask them to hold their jumper in the air. Then send Tom outside the room for a moment. Meanwhile, everyone takes off their jumpers and holds them in the air – and then bring Tom back in again for the surprising end to the story.

The Contented Priest

This works well with a few props. You could put on a big hoody when the gardener docs. You could drop a few coins when the gardener gives his answer to the first question. You could stamp on the floor when the gardener answers the second question. And you could throw back the hood when the gardener answers the final question. As far as your audience participation is concerned, they could repeat the three questions after you, whenever they come up in the story.

Olle and the Troll

Use the hoody from the previous story for this one as well. First, ask your audience to make troll faces and grunting troll noises with you. Squash your nose to your face or put your fingers over your eyebrows and wiggle them. Draw a big imaginary line from ear to ear and make a scary smile. And shake your left hand and howl like a wolf. You might want to repeat these actions every time the story says, "Olle had never seen a troll."

Then put on the hoody and, pretending to be the troll, wrap a bit of cloth around that wolf hand. And when the troll laughs at the end, rock your head back and laugh out loud, and then splutter and choke when the bread is popped into your mouth.

The Steel Man

Everyone plays Joe Magarac, repeating the actions after you as appropriate. They stamp on the floor (Boom! Boom! Boom!), make a rumbling tumbling laugh and hee-haw like donkeys. They also pretend to gobble up coal and drink steel soup and pick their teeth with chisels, then pick up the railroad tracks, and stir and squeeze the steel in their fists to make the beams. As the steelworkers search the mill for Joe, they can all laugh along with you.

The Crafty Farmer

Your audience can climb the pole with Farmer Yasohachi. Make climbing motions – perhaps taking them from a seating to a crouching to a standing position – and then all fall down!

Tiger Tries to Cheat

You play Tiger and two children play the cave, making an arch with their arms above you. Another child plays the boulder, standing in front of you. Everyone else pretends to be the other animals, pushing and grunting in their seats. Then simply reverse the motions when Tortoise makes his suggestion at the end.

The Two Brothers

The audience play the wasps in the wasps' nest, making a buzzing sounds and waving their hands about whenever the wasps or the nest are mentioned.

Kayoku and the Crane

This is quite a serious story, so any silly participation will only spoil the mood. But the audience can call like a crane – a long, sad "aaw-aaw" – both at the start and at the end when the crane flies away.

The Two Sisters

Divide your audience in half. One group plays the kind daughter, repeating her kind words and actions after you. The other group plays the unkind daughter, similarly repeating her words and actions. It's also fun to have two bags – one filled with plastic flowers and cheap jewellery, and the other with rubber snakes and frogs – to toss on the floor at the appropriate times!

The Selfish Beasts

Divide your group into three parts – one for each animal. The Lion group roars, the Hyena group yip-yaps, and the Vulture group squawks. Bring them all in together while they chew on the antelope at the beginning. Then bring them in whenever the animals describe their pet peeves, when they fight, and then, one by one, as they eat alone at the end.

The Determined Frog

Everyone joins in the frog's words with you: "I can't give up and I won't give up!" They can also move their legs and arms in a paddling motion, getting more desperate and loud as the frog's struggles increase. They could also join you in a "splish and splash and jump and croak" action.

The Robber and the Monk

Choose three volunteers – one to be the monk, one to be the robber and one to be the shopkeeper. Find a big book and pass it from one to the other at the appropriate times.

The Fox and the Crow

You play the fox and have your crowd play the crow, scratching their heads when she is confused, smiling when she is flattered, trembling when she does, but all the while keeping their mouths shut very tightly. Then have the crowd let out an awful "squawk"when crow tries to sing.

City Mouse and Country Mouse

Have everyone make car sounds, and maybe even turn a pretend steering wheel. Have them go "beep-beep" when Mouse's car is moving through town, then a quiet "humm" when it goes a little more quickly in the suburbs, then a throaty "roar" when Mouse speeds through the country.

   You can also divide them into three groups – one to make cat sounds, one to make dog sounds, and one to make the "snap" of the mouse trap.

Why the Cat Falls on Her Feet

Make this a counting story. Teach everyone the numbers and the sounds ahead of time.

   When Eagle is mentioned, have everyone hold up two fingers and "screech". For Snake, have everyone make a "zero" with their thumb and forefinger and "hiss". Spider – eight fingers and a "scrickety-scrackety" sound. Possum – one finger and a big yawn. Ant – six fingers and a grunt. Cat – four fingers in a claw shape and a noisy "meow".

Big Jack, Little Jack and the Donkey

Have everyone say "That is the silliest thing I ever saw!" in five different voices – the old woman, the old man, the girl, the boy, and the mayor. Teach them the voices ahead of time.

   As an option, you might divide the crowd into five groups, one for each of the voices.

The Lion's Advice

Have your group play the lion, roaring, growling, and sniffing when he does.

The Dog and the Wolf

Have everyone play the dog. Growl when he growls. Gobble up the dog food with him (maybe a big "Mmm" at the end!). Curl up and fall to sleep with him (doggy snores). Lie in front of the fireplace (contented doggy sighs). And maybe lots of panting and happy yipping when he talks about playing with the farmer. But when the dog mentions the collar, have everyone tug at their collars. And when he mentions the chain, have everyone try to move and get jerked back.

Practice the motions and sounds ahead of time.

The Kind Parrot

Have everyone say the first line of the "parrot poems" with you in a squawky parrot voice.

The Tortoise and the Hare

Divide your group into two. Have one half play the hare – hands for ears, buck-toothed, and beating the floor with their feet every time Hare runs. Have the other half play the tortoise – jumpers and tops pulled up under their noses for shells, and moving their hands and feet very very slowly.

If you'd rather not pitch them against each other, you can also have everyone play the tortoise and the hare!

Why Dogs Chase Cats and Cats Chase Mice

Divide your group into three – dogs, cats, and mice. Have the dog group do what the dogs do in the story – woofing, yipping, yapping, wagging tales, scratching, and barking. Have the cat group stretch and meow and purr. And have the mice group nibble and nibble and nibble!

Rabbit and the Briar Patch

Have everyone join the rabbit in saying, "But please, oh please, don't chuck me into that briar patch!" Use a squeaky little voice, with a southern drawl, if you can. Have everyone scream and shout with the rabbit, as well, when he's in the briar patch.

The Crocodile Brother

Divide your crowd into three groups. Have one group play the crocodile, grinning, opening their mouths wide, and snapping their jaws shut with a growl. Have another group play the chicken, clucking when the chicken is mentioned, and saying, in a chicken voice, "My brother, please spare my life. Find something else for your supper." Have the last group play the duck, quacking when the duck is mentioned, and saying, in a duck voice, "My brother, please spare my life. Find something else for your supper."

The Boastful Toad

Divide your crowd into four groups. Have the first group boast, "I can jump much higher than you!" while jumping in the air. Have the second group boast, "I can kill more flies than you!" while sticking out their tongues like frogs and slurping up pretend flies. Have the third group boast, "I can swim much further than you!" while making frog-swimming motions. Have the fourth group boast, "I can make myself bigger than you!" while sucking in a big breath of air. And then have everyone suck in big breaths of air along with the boastful toad.

The Clever Mouse Deer

Have everyone make elephant, pig, and ape noises at the beginning of the story.

The Ant and the Grasshopper

Lead everyone in a big yawn and then, with a sleepy voice, have them say Grasshopper's line with you: "Come and sit with me for a while!" You'll need to do it in a shivery voice the final time. Have them say "Can't" with Ant in a sharp and squeaky little voice, as well.

You could divide the group into two instead, and have one group play Grasshopper and the other play Ant.

Big Jack, Little Jack and the Farmer

Have your group play Farmer Fred, whooping and hollering with him in the first part of the story, making vrooming car noises and splashing swimming noises in the second part, and weeping and wailing noises in the last part.

Three Days of the Dragon

Have everyone roar, "The Legends!" when the dragon does. And have them jump up and down like they are the children on the dragon's belly.

How the Turkey Got Its Spots

Divide your group into two. Have one group play the lion – creeping and leaping and roaring and coughing and sneezing with him. Have the other group play the turkey, scratching and flapping and gobble-gobbling.

The Tortoise and the Fox

Have everyone play the tortoise, pulling their tops or jumpers up under their noses when he disappears inside his shell, shuddering and shivering with him when Leopard tries to get inside, and then sneaking away when he reaches the river bed.

The Generous Rabbit

Have everyone shiver and sneeze and walk through the snow with Rabbit (hopping, hands like ears), Donkey (hee-hawing, hands like ears as well), Sheep (baa-ing), and Squirrel (hand waving like bushy tail from behind) motions and voices.

The Noble Rooster

Have everyone "Cock-a-doodle-do!" with the rooster.

Rabbit and the Crops

You might want to make three simple props for this one. Use three large pieces of paper or card. Fold the first paper in half. Draw potatoes on the bottom half, and potato leaves on the top. Fold the second paper in half as well. Draw oat stalks on the bottom half, and oats on the top. Fold the third piece into thirds! Draw corn stalks on the bottom and leaves on the top. And put ears of sweetcorn in the middle. Then use them to tell the story.

The Woman and the Bird

Choose a volunteer or two or three to dance like the bird. Teach them a silly little dance – or let them make up their own. And have them dance every time the bird does.

The Mole's Bridegroom

Lead your group in playing the sun (make circle with arms and shout, "Shine!"), the sky (wave hands in sky and shout, "Sky!"), the clouds (point in the air and say, "Puffy!"), the wind (wave hands back and forth and say, "Whooo!"), and the earth (stomp feet and say in deep voice, "Earth!").

The Kind-hearted Crocodile

Divide your crowd into five groups. Have one group shout, "Dingos are for dinner!" The second group, "Roos are for stews!" The third group, "Koalas are for kebabing!" The fourth group, "Goannas are for garnishing!" The last group, "Platypuses are for pickling!"

Why the Tortoise Has No Hair

Have everyone make a rumbly tummy sound with the tortoise. Have them make a dribbly drooly sound with the tortoise. Have them slurp up the porridge with the tortoise. And then lead them in a big sigh when the tortoise looks into his hat at the end.

Big Jack, Little Jack and the Bird

Big Jack and Little Jack speak in couplets in this story. So divide your group into two. Have the first group repeat what Big Jack says after you, in a deep Big Jack voice. And have the second group repeat what Little Jack says, in a squeaky Little Jack voice.

It might also be fun to have a volunteer play the bird and several others to play all the "bad" Jacks, and then to have them link up and race around the room.

How the Rabbit Lost Its Tail

Have everyone turn their arm into the rabbit's tail: dragging it in a long, wavy motion; sticking it straight up into the air; making it bounce up and down. And when the tail is bitten off – turning the hand into a fist.

You could also make this a counting story and have everyone count the sharks with you in groups of ten. Practice it ahead of time.

The Badger Teapot

Divide your crowd into three groups. Have the first group make the "Ting-a-ling. Clang-clang. Plonkety-plonk" sound with you. Have the second group shout, "Hot! Hot! Much too hot!" with the badger. Have the third group clap and cheer with the crowd.

The Kind of Hungry Lion

Have everyone growl along with the lion's tummy, getting louder as it does.

The Big, Soft, Fluffy Bed

Have everyone "squeeeek" with the door, cry ("Boo-hoo-hoo") with Danny, "miaow" with the cat, "woof" with the dog, "oink" with the pig, and "neigh" with the pony. And you could have them snore with Danny at the end as well, when he finally goes to sleep!

The Peanut Boy

There's a little chorus to the story that builds as the story goes on. Teach your group the sounds and actions to that chorus and lead them along the way:

"Henry in a peanut shell": they scrunch up their faces, or surround a fist with an open hand. "Henry in a chicken": make a chicken sound. "Henry in a sly old fox": yipping sound. "Henry in a hungry wolf": howl. "Henry in a great big fish": glub. And Henry's mum and Henry's dad just talking in the kitchen: make talking hands.

The Wonderful Bird

Have everyone make the "Kekeko. Kekeko" (the accent is on the first syllable, I think!) sound with you. And have them say her name with you when it appears.

The Cat, the Mice and the Cheese

Have everyone play the mice – squeaking and squabbling in little mice voices whenever the mice do.

The Goats and the Hyena

Divide your crowd into three groups. Teach the first group the line "They are my horns, sir." And have them make horns on their heads with their fingers. The second group, "It is my woolly coat, sir." And have them wrap their arms around themselves. The third group, "Because I am afraid that you will eat me, sir." And have them chomp their teeth. Do all the lines in a na-a-a-ing goat voice. Then lead them in those lines when the first two goats answer the hyena.

The Clever Crows

You might like to use this as a maths/counting story, depending on the age of your group. So you could ask them to give the answer to the "adding up the pebbles" question.

   You could also use coloured marbles for the pebbles and actually make the water rise in a bottle by adding them according to the story.

The Monkeys and the Mangoes

Ask your group what their favourite food is. Then tell them your favourite food and explain that whenever you think of your favourite food, you rub your tummy and go "Mmm". Tell them to think of their favourite food and say "Mmm" together. Then lead them in that sound whenever it appears in the story.

A note from the author

Most of the stories in this book are retellings of traditional tales from around the world. They have been retold by many people over the years and I am just the next in a long line of storytellers. Each of us uses slightly different words and phrases, and so the stories evolve. You may wish to read other versions of some of these stories, so I would like to acknowledge some of the sources I have referred to, although most of these stories can be found in several collections. You will find the stories listed under the titles used in this book, but they should be easy to identify in the books I mention.

Three Months' Night from 'One Night, One Day' in *Tales of the Nimipoo* by E.B. Heady, World Publishing Co, New York. **Arion and the Dolphin** from 'The Boy and the Dolphin' in *Old Greek Fairy Tales* by R. Lancelyn Green, G. Bell & Sons Ltd, London. The **Rabbit and Tiger** stories from *The Tiger and the Rabbit and Other Tales* by P. Belpre, J.B. Lippincott & Co. **The Shepherd and the Clever Princess** from 'Timo and the Princess Vendla' and **The Amazing Pine Cone** from 'The Two Pine Cones' in *Tales from a Finnish Tupa* by J. Lloyd Bowman and M. Blanco, A. Whitman & Co, Chicago. **Tortoise Brings Food** from 'Uwungelema' and **The Very Strong Sparrow** from 'The Strongest Sparrow in the Forest' in *African Fairy Tales* by K. Arnott, Frederick Muller Ltd, London. **The Mouse Deer's Wisdom** from 'King Solomon, the Merchant and the Mouse Deer' in *Java Jungle Tales* by H. DeLeeuw, Arco Publishing, New York. **The Four Friends** from 'The Goat, the Raven, the Rat, and the Tortoise' in *Animal Folk Tales* by B. Kerr Wilson, Hamlyn Publishing Group, London. **The Brave Bull Calf** from 'A Little Bull Calf' in *The Gypsy Fiddle* by J. Hampden, World Publishing Co, New York. **The Clever Mouse** from 'St Cadog and the Mouse' in *Welsh Legendary Tales* by E. Sheppard-Jones, Nelson, Edinburgh. **The Selfish Sand Frog** from 'The Thirsty Sand Frog' and **How the Kangaroo Got Its Tail** in *Djugurba: Tales from the Spirit Time*, Australian National University Press, Canberra. **The Mouse's Bride** from *Fairy Tales of India* by L. Turnbull, Criterion Books, New York. **The Big Wave** from *Gleanings in Buddha Fields* by Lafcadio Hearn, Houghton Mifflin Co, Boston. **The Knee-High Man** from 'The Knee-High Man' in *The Stars Fell on Alabama* by C. Carmer, Farrar and Rinehart, New York. **The Clever Baker** from 'The Woman Who Flummoxed the Fairies' in *Heather and Broom* by S.N. Leodhas, Holt, Rinehart, and Winston, New York. **The Greedy Farmer** from 'The Marvellous Cow of Clyn Barfog' in *Elves and Ellefolk* by N.M. Belting, Holt, Rinehart, and Winston, New York. **Lazy Tom** from 'The Field of Boliauns' in *Fairy Tales from the British Isles* by A. Williams-Ellis, Frederick Warne & Co, London. **The Contented Priest** from 'The Gardener, the Abbot and the King' in *Bungling Pedro and Other Majorcan Tales* by A. Mehdevi, Alfred A. Knopf, New York. **Olle and the Troll** from 'The Old Troll of the Big Mountain' in *The Faber Book of Northern Folktales* by K. Crossley-Holland, Faber & Faber, London. **The Steel Man** from *Joe Magarac and His USA Citizen Papers* by I. Shapiro, University of Pittsburgh Press, Pittsburgh. **The Crafty Farmer** from 'Crafty Yasohachi Climbs to Heaven' and **Kayoku and the Crane** from 'The Cloth of a Thousand Feathers' in *Men from the Village Deep in the Mountains*, translated by G. Bang, Collier Macmillan Publishers, London. **The Two Brothers** from

'The Golden Gourd' in *South American Wonder Tales* by F. Carpenter, Follett Publishing Company, New York. **The Selfish Beasts** from 'Why the Lion, the Vulture, and the Hyena Do Not Live Together' in *Olode the Hunter and Other Tales from Nigeria* by H. Courlander, Harcourt, Brace & World Inc, New York. **The Determined Frog** from 'The Wise Frog and the Foolish Frog' in *Tales of Central Russia* by J. Riordan, Kestrel Books, London. **The Robber and the Monk** from *The Desert Fathers*, translated by H. Waddell, Collins Publishers, London. **The Peanut Boy** and **The Big, Soft, Fluffy Bed** from *10 Small Tales*, Celia Barker Lottridge, Margaret K. McElderry Books, NY, 1994. **The Fox and the Crow**, **The Tortoise and the Hare**, **Big Jack, Little Jack and the Donkey**, **Big Jack, Little Jack and the Farmer** and **The Dog and the Wolf** from *Aesop* or from *The Fables of La Fontaine*, Richard Scarry, Doubleday and Company Inc., Garden City NY 1963. **The Goats and the Hyena** from *Arab Folktales*, ed. Inea Bushnaq, Pantheon Books, NY 1986. **The Mole's Bridegroom** from *Asian-Pacific Folktales and Legends*, ed. Jeannette Faurot, Touchstone, NY 1995. **Big Jack, Little Jack and the Bird** from *A Book of Cats and Creatures*. **City Mouse and Country Mouse**, **The Boastful Toad**, **The Ant and the Grasshopper** and **The Clever Crows** from *Folk Lore and Fable*, The Harvard Classics, ed. Charles W. Eliot, P.F.Collier and Son Company, NY 1909. **Why the Cat Falls on Her Feet** and **Why Dogs Chase Cats and Cats Chase Mice** from *The Folktale Cat*, Frank de Caro, Barnes and Noble Books, NY 1992. **The Tortoise and the Fox** from *Folktales from India*, A. K. Ramanujan, Pantheon Books, NY 1991. **The Clever Mouse Deer** and **The Wonderful Bird** from *Indonesian Fairy Tales*, Adele deLeeuw, Frederick Muller Limited, London. **The Monkeys and the Mangoes** from *The Jataka Tales*. **How the Rabbit Lost Its Tail** and

The Noble Rooster from *Little One-Inch and Other Japanese Children's Favorite Stories*, ed. Florence Sakade, Charles E. Tuttle Company, Rutland, Vermont, 1984 **The Generous Rabbit** from *The Rabbit and the Turnip*, tr. Richard Sadler, Doubleday and Company Inc., Garden City NY, 1968. **How the Turkey Got Its Spots** and **The Woman and the Bird** from *Tales from the African Plains*, Anne Gatti, Pavilion Books, London, 1994. **Rabbit and the Briar Patch** and **Rabbit and the Crops** from *A Treasury of American Folklore*, ed. B.A.Botkin, Crown Publishers, NY 1944. **The Cat, the Mice and the Cheese** from *A Treasury of Jewish Folklore*, ed. Nathan Ausubel, Crown Publishers, NY 1975. **The Lion's Advice**, **Why Tortoise Has No Hair** and **The Kind Parrot** from *West African Folk Tales*, Jack Berry, Northwestern University Press, Evanston Illinois 1991. **The Crocodile Brother** from *Zoo of the Gods*, Anthony S. Mercatante, Harper and Row, NY 1974.